Praise for
Carlton Mellick III

"Easily the craziest, weirdest, strangest, funniest, most obscene writer in America."
—*GOTHIC MAGAZINE*

"Carlton Mellick III has the craziest book titles... and the kinkiest fans!"
—CHRISTOPHER MOORE, author of *The Stupidest Angel*

"If you haven't read Mellick you're not nearly perverse enough for the twenty first century."
—JACK KETCHUM, author of *The Girl Next Door*

"Carlton Mellick III is one of bizarro fiction's most talented practitioners, a virtuoso of the surreal, science fictional tale."
—CORY DOCTOROW, author of *Little Brother*

"Bizarre, twisted, and emotionally raw—Carlton Mellick's fiction is the literary equivalent of putting your brain in a blender."
—BRIAN KEENE, author of *The Rising*

"Carlton Mellick III exemplifies the intelligence and wit that lurks between its lurid covers. In a genre where crude titles are an art in themselves, Mellick is a true artist."
—*THE GUARDIAN*

"Just as Pop had Andy Warhol and Dada Tristan Tzara, the bizarro movement has its very own P. T. Barnum-type practitioner. He's the mutton-chopped author of such books as *Electric Jesus Corpse* and *The Menstruating Mall*, the illustrator, editor, and instructor of all things bizarro, and his name is Carlton Mellick III."
—*DETAILS MAGAZINE*

Also by
Carlton Mellick III

Satan Burger
Electric Jesus Corpse (Fan Club Exclusive)
Sunset With a Beard (stories)
Razor Wire Pubic Hair
Teeth and Tongue Landscape
The Steel Breakfast Era
The Baby Jesus Butt Plug
Fishy-fleshed
The Menstruating Mall
Ocean of Lard (with Kevin L. Donihe)
Punk Land
Sex and Death in Television Town
Sea of the Patchwork Cats
The Haunted Vagina
Cancer-cute (Fan Club Exclusive)
War Slut
Sausagey Santa
Ugly Heaven
Adolf in Wonderland
Ultra Fuckers
Cybernetrix
The Egg Man
Apeshit
The Faggiest Vampire
The Cannibals of Candyland
Warrior Wolf Women of the Wasteland
The Kobold Wizard's Dildo of Enlightenment +2
Zombies and Shit
Crab Town
The Morbidly Obese Ninja
Barbarian Beast Bitches of the Badlands
Fantastic Orgy (stories)

SCORPION
RANCH

CARLTON MELLICK III

ERASERHEAD PRESS
PORTLAND, OREGON

ERASERHEAD PRESS
205 NE BRYANT
PORTLAND, OR 97211

WWW.ERASERHEADPRESS.COM

ISBN: 978-1-62105-364-4

Copyright © 2025 by Carlton Mellick III

Cover art copyright © 2025 Anton Vilkin

Printed in the USA.

AUTHOR'S NOTE

Everyone in my hometown is named Marvin. I'm not sure why. It's not a very common name. And yet here I am the only Carlton in a town full of Marvins. I guess there is one Lyle. He lives just outside of town near the gas station. He never comes very far into town though. Something about all the Marvins gives me the creeps. The way they all go to sleep at the exact same time every night and wake up at 4am every single morning. The way they sometimes stare at me through my windows at night with their wide round eyes. There's just something not quite right about them. I've been thinking about changing my name to Marvin just to be on the safe side.

—Carlton Mellick III   10/22/2024 9:10pm

CHAPTER
ONE

Daniel Munch is dating a scorpion. Well, she's not a *real* scorpion. In fact, it's kind of racist to call her that. But she does belong to a new race of women who have developed poison glands in their mouths and vaginas. Nobody knows why some women have evolved into venomous creatures. Some people think it was just a random genetic mutation. Others speculate it developed specifically to be a natural defense against sexual predators. If a man ever attempts to assault a woman with poisonous vaginal fluids, he would be dead within minutes. This quickly made rape a very rare occurrence in our culture because it encouraged men to think twice about sleeping with any woman, especially a stranger who would see him as a threat. Some scorpion women look no different from other human women, but others are born with aposematism—brightly colored skin intended to warn predators of their venomous nature. Their skin is a warning message to all those who would attack them. And that message is: Eat me if you dare.

Daniel's girlfriend has aposematism. When he first met her, he was shocked by the colors of her skin. Her face is ruby red, with inky black spots scattered around her eyes and down her neck. Her arms and chest are streaked with electric blue, and her fingertips glow maize yellow. She looks like some kind of poison frog from the Amazon rainforest, despite otherwise being human.

They met through an online dating app and scheduled their date the same week. However, Daniel had no idea he'd been matched with a scorpion. She hadn't mentioned it in her profile. Even her picture was different. She looked like a perfectly normal girl—nice, approachable, and stunningly attractive. Daniel could hardly believe someone so beautiful would be willing to go on a date with him. Of course, there had to be a catch.

When the brightly colored woman came up to him, she held out her hand to shake, "You're Daniel, right? I'm Sora." She had a thick Tennessee accent, despite looking like the kind of person who grew up in an urban California city her whole life.

Daniel stood there, confused for a moment, but shook her hand anyway.

"Um… hello," he responded, staring down at her brightly colored fingers wrapped around his hand.

He'd dated heavily tattooed girls before, even girls who were trying to pass themselves off as scorpions by giving themselves tattoos in similar patterns, but the real thing was much different. The colors were more vibrant than any tattoo ink. And the texture of her skin felt oddly smooth and alien to him. She seemed dangerous to touch.

"Sorry, I kind of catfished you," she said as they sat down at a table in the back corner of the brewery. Daniel noticed the nearby patrons fall quiet, eyes darting over in wary glances, as though he'd walked in with a wild animal. "I put my photo through a filter that changed my skin tone. It's the only way I ever get any dates these days. Nobody wants to go out with a venomous woman—especially one who looks like me."

Daniel just nodded, unsure what to say. People were openly staring now, their eyes flicking from her to him, equal parts fear and bewilderment in their faces. They watched her as if they needed to keep her in sight, just in case she touched anything they might want to touch. They kept their eyes on Daniel, too—they were either concerned for his safety or questioning his sanity for going out to dinner with a scorpion. Sora could tell it was making him feel awkward, she'd seen it many times before. She was obviously used to being treated like a dangerous freak of nature.

"Does it bother you?" she asked.

Daniel shrugged. "I don't know. I've never been on a date with a scorpion before."

She shot him an annoyed look at his use of the term *scorpion*, but quickly let it slide. Despite being an offensive racial slur, it was so commonplace that even venomous women usually used the term to describe themselves.

"We're not as dangerous as they say," Sora told him. "By eighteen, we have complete control over our venom glands. We only poison men who deserve it."

Daniel wasn't exactly reassured.

"All the accidental deaths are from younger girls—teenagers who haven't fully mastered it yet," she went on, unfazed by his unease. "Some release it unintentionally, especially during orgasm."

Daniel shifted uncomfortably in his seat. Sitting across from her felt surreal—like he was on a date with a gorgon or a werewolf. But he was also a bit intrigued. He knew very little about women like her.

"Have you ever poisoned somebody by accident before?" Daniel asked.

She looked away briefly before nodding. "Once. Not during sex though. By law, we're not allowed to date until we turn eighteen. Even kissing a guy could kill him. Even sharing the same cup."

"So who did you poison?"

"My brother," she said, a hint of regret in her voice. "It was a stupid mistake. I was masturbating one day and didn't realize I got my venom on my fingers. It clung to everything I touched—the bathroom doorknob, the kitchen cabinets, even the counter where my brother made his peanut butter sandwiches. He must have gotten some on his hand while he was making himself a snack." She shook her head slightly. "He was lucky, though. He didn't ingest much of it and my family always kept some anti-venom on hand."

"There's anti-venom for your poison?" Daniel's eyebrows shot up. This was news to him.

Sora shrugged. "Yes, but it usually doesn't work. Our poison is the most deadly on the planet. The anti-venom only works on very small amounts of the poison and has to be injected immediately after exposure. Most of the time it's just too little too late. But it's mandatory for families with poisonous children to keep some on hand."

The waiter approached with their drinks. He carefully set both on Daniel's side of the table, keeping as much distance from Sora as possible, his eyes fixed on the scorpion as if she might lunge.

After the waiter hurried off, Daniel asked, "How did your family take it after you poisoned your brother?"

Sora let out a dry laugh. "The police told my parents they had to make a choice," she said, her gaze fixed upon the table. "Either my brother would be placed in foster care or I'd be sent off to the Scorpion Ranch." She glanced back at Daniel, "They chose my brother."

"What's the Scorpion Ranch?"

"It's a nickname for the detention center where they send girls like me, the ones who can't control their poison," Sora said, her tone turning flat, as if she were stating a simple fact. "I spent the rest of my childhood surrounded by murderers."

Daniel raised an eyebrow. "Murderers? Is it really murder if you kill someone by accident because you can't control your poison?"

Sora's lips curled in a humorless smile. "Most of them were murderers by accident. But some of them would kill men on purpose. It was a control thing. The idea that they could kill a man whenever they wanted was a thrill to some scorpion women. The black widows, we called them. They got off on poisoning their boyfriends when they had sex with them and then pretended they just couldn't control it, playing the victim to get away with murder. They found it exciting and empowering."

She shook her head, a bitterness creeping into her voice. "I hated girls like that. They make it so much harder for the rest of us, because now everyone thinks all venomous women are crazy and dangerous like them."

Daniel hesitated, searching her face for a moment. "So you're not crazy and dangerous?" he asked.

Sora let out a genuine laugh, the sound echoing through the quiet corner of the bar. She thought he was joking around. "Oh, I'm definitely crazy and dangerous! Even without my venom."

Although he could tell she was being playful, it did nothing to ease Daniel's nerves.

It was a very awkward first date. Daniel didn't really think he related to her at all. They didn't like a lot of the same things and hated each other's taste in music. Daniel's favorite band was *The Pogues* and her favorite band was *Die Antwoord*. Even though they were only four years apart, they belonged to different generations and it showed. Talking about their upbringings and cultural differences made Daniel feel like an old man.

Still, Daniel didn't hate spending the evening with her and she said she had a good time as well. They didn't fall instantly in love, but they weren't put off by each other, either. Daniel had been single for so long that he was lonely and in need of companionship, and Sora admitted she'd been so isolated, so avoided by everyone, that it was driving her crazy.

On their second date, Sora confided that she had tried

dating other scorpions in the past.

"It's really the only way to date somebody who feels completely safe with you," she said. "Scorpions can't poison each other, so we don't think of each other as dangerous. That's why so many of us are lesbians. I tried dating other scorpion women for a while, but it's not for me. I'm just not into girls."

"Too bad there aren't any male scorpions," Daniel said.

She shook her head. "The world's probably better off without male scorpions. A man who can inject poison into women with his penis? Way more people would die, on purpose and by accident. It'd be a nightmare for non-venomous women." She gave a small shrug. "Though I guess the name *scorpion* would make a lot more sense if men were venomous."

Daniel didn't realize she was comparing a venomous man's penis to a scorpion tail.

"How many people have you dated?" he asked, not sure why he'd ask something so personal. She didn't seem put off by the question.

"Well, I've gone on dozens of dates. But I've only had three serious relationships Two men and one woman. I was with the woman the longest but… she was too clingy and I wasn't really attracted to her." She paused, glancing down at her yellow fingers. "One guy I was deeply in love with—probably a little too much. I wanted to marry him." Her voice softened. "But that scared him away. He thought about what it would be like having children with somebody like me and decided it was too complicated for him. He didn't want to deal with the dangers of having a venomous daughter. I told him we didn't have to have kids but he knew it was a lie. He said I needed to find a guy who was willing to have children with me despite the consequences. He's married now and has a beautiful daughter. I'm happy for him. Really, I am."

Daniel realized it was a sensitive topic for her. He noticed her eyes glisten slightly as she spoke, her voice tinged with a sadness that he hadn't seen in her before. The memory of being rejected by someone she'd loved clearly still hurt. So he decided to change the subject.

"What about the other guy?" he asked.

She laughed, wiping a tear from her ruby cheek. "Oh, that guy. He was a freak." She took a sip of her beer. "He was the last guy I dated. He had a scorpion fetish."

"A scorpion fetish?"

"Some guys are into us because of our skin colors," she said, rolling her eyes. "And instead of being frightened by our venom glands, they are turned on by them." She took a sip of her beer, before going on. "This guy actually wanted me to poison him. He thought it would be the sexiest thing in the world to be fucked to death by a scorpion. Can you believe that?" She shook her head, almost laughing at the memory. "I dated him for a year, honestly, just because I was lonely and horny. And sex with a guy who had absolutely no hesitation whatsoever was kind of great, I'm not gonna lie." She sighed, her expression tightening. "But obviously, that wasn't going to last. There was no way I was going to give him what he wanted."

Sora's expression hardened. "He even tried to rape me once, thinking he could force me to poison him, but I fought him off without using it. I beat the absolute shit out of him and got a restraining order. I hope I never see that guy for the rest of my life."

"Seems like you've had it rough," Daniel said quietly.

Sora raised an eyebrow, a glint of humor in her eyes. "What about you? Have you had any shitty relationships?"

Daniel hesitated. He didn't like talking about himself very much, especially not his love life. But since he had been prying into her sordid past, he felt it would only be fair to be completely honest.

"A few," he said, nodding while taking a sip. "I seem to have a thing for vengeful women."

"Vengeful?"

Sora seemed amused.

"Yeah," He let out a short laugh. "I broke up with one woman and she set my car on fire. Apparently, she didn't like my reason for ending things."

"What reason was that?"

"She had two kids, and I said I wasn't ready to be a father. She was cool with it at first—at least when we started dating. I told her that I wasn't willing to get serious with her because of that. But she didn't accept it. She said that I had to marry her or break up with her and I chose the latter. She was not happy about that one bit."

"What about the others?"

He sighed, setting his glass down. "Well, one woman broke up with me but for some reason still decided to get back at me by putting revenge porn of me online."

Sora's eyebrows shot up. "Revenge porn?"

He nodded, a bit more wary this time. "Yeah. She was into filming me... naked. You know, doing things—masturbating, sucking on my fingers, us having sex. She'd always film it from her perspective, so she wouldn't be on camera. She said she did it because there wasn't enough good porn for women online and so she had to make her own. But now I wonder if she did it to control or to get revenge on boyfriends who pissed her off." He paused, grimacing. "I'm not sure. Anyway, she left me for another guy, and when I started dating somebody else, she got mad and posted the videos online. I've had some taken down, but I'm sure there are still a bunch out there somewhere."

Sora seemed very amused by his story. "I had no idea I was dating a porn star."

"It's not funny," Daniel said. "I was so embarrassed. I felt so... violated. Who knows how many people have seen those videos..."

"Hey," she said, giving him a sympathetic look. "It's actually kind of cool that you were willing to make those videos for her. I've never met a guy who'd be willing to do that."

He shrugged. "I completely regret it though."

Sora grinned. "You just dated the wrong person. A guy who's willing to go out of his comfort zone to explore a woman's kinks is pretty rare. My respect for you just went up tenfold."

Daniel didn't know how to take her compliment. He wasn't sure if he should be happy or annoyed that she was impressed by the most humiliating moment of his life.

"If it makes you feel any better, there's videos of me online too," Sora said after a sip of hefeweizen. "I used to be a camgirl. Guys might be afraid to date venomous women, but aposematic girls like me are really popular in the sex industry. A lot of us end up as nude models, strippers or cam girls. Strippers don't make that much money because nobody wants a lap dance from us, but a good OnlyFans page can make decent money."

Daniel didn't know what to think. It was already awkward to date a scorpion. Dating one who also did porn was a bit too much. He was pretty sure he could never get serious with a woman like her.

"Do you still do it?" he asked, trying to keep his tone casual.

She shook her head. "Maybe a photoset here and there, but I took down my OnlyFans page years ago. It was too much of a grind and got way too competitive. There are too many women with aposematism these days and most of them have far prettier colors than I do. Having blue boobs isn't good enough anymore."

Maybe he had too many beers, but her words perked Daniel up a bit. He found himself asking, "You have blue boobs?"

"Yeah, totally." She pulled her shirt down a few inches, revealing bright sapphire-blue cleavage. Her skin had a glossy sheen, catching the light, and Daniel couldn't tell if it was from sweat or just her natural texture. "I think I got lucky. My ex-girlfriend had black and yellow boobs that made her look like she had wasp butts on her chest. They weren't nearly as attractive as mine."

She pulled her shirt back up, smiling as she met his gaze. Daniel's face grew hot, and he quickly looked away. She was much less inhibited than other girls he'd dated.

"Want to go back to my place after this?" she asked. "I live within walking distance."

"Sure," Daniel said, without thinking.

It took him a few minutes before he realized that she was inviting him back to her place to have sex with him.

Daniel had no intention of sleeping with a scorpion. That was just way too risky for him, no matter how drunk and horny he was. It had been over a year since he'd been with a woman and he just wasn't desperate enough to put his life on the line for sex. But he wasn't going to change his plans with Sora. He was still willing to go back to her place since he already agreed to it and thought it would be awkward to change his mind on her, but that was all he was willing to do. He didn't actually agree to sleep with her and maybe she really did just want to watch a movie or listen to some music or something.

As they walked down the city street, everyone avoided them. Even at night, a scorpion's brightly colored skin could be seen from three blocks away. Groups of people would cross the street so they wouldn't have to pass her on the same sidewalk. An old married couple turned a corner to avoid them. Even a methhead street punk hid in his tent and closed the flaps tightly as they passed by.

Both of them realized what was happening, but Daniel was the only one who seemed bothered by it.

"Is it always this way?" he asked her.

She nodded her head. "I don't mind when people avoid me. I kind of like it, to be honest. What I don't like is the people who get in my face and start a fight with me."

"Like who?"

Sora shrugged. "Drunk assholes will call me a scorpion

cunt and tell me to fuck off for no reason. Rightwing psychos who think we're spawns of the devil will get in my face and tell me to go back to hell where I belong. But the worst are women whose sons died as teenagers from sleeping with one of my kind. A lot of them blame all of us for their children's death. I feel bad for them, but people like that want all of us to be put behind bars."

"Can't you get your poison glands removed?" Daniel asked. "If you did that, then you wouldn't be seen as dangerous to anyone."

Sora froze mid-step. She turned to him slowly, her eyes burning with intensity, unblinking as if she were daring him to provoke her further. "Are you fucking kidding me? How could you say that?" Her voice was sharp and dangerous. "Do you know how inhumane that is? Asshole *male* politicians have been trying to make that mandatory for years." She crossed her arms, eyes narrowing to slits. "They even talked about sterilizing us. Sterilizing us so no other venomous women would be born." She shook her head. "And it doesn't even make sense—you don't have to be a scorpion mother in order to have scorpion kids. It's so fucking racist."

Daniel felt horrible about having said that. He tried to take it back. "I'm sorry, I had no idea. I don't think forcing scorpions to remove their venom sack is cool at all."

She completely ignored his apology, especially since he used the term *scorpion* to do it. "All the people who want our glands removed are just misogynistic men who want to have sex with us without worry of being poisoned. It's like they're pissed off they can't safely rape anyone they want anymore. Fuck those assholes."

Daniel just nodded his head and kept his mouth shut.

Sora took them down a side street to get to her apartment when a man in a black hoodie and facemask jumped in front of them, blocking their path.

A knife glinted in his hand. "Give me everything you got!"

Daniel laughed when he saw the guy. He thought the man had to be joking. He knew that crime had been escalating downtown, but he never heard of anyone getting mugged before. He thought that was something that only happened in old movies.

"I'm not fucking around!" the man shouted, his hand shaking as he pointed the knife.

Daniel stopped laughing. Seeing how twitchy the guy was, he realized it wasn't a joke. They were really being mugged.

"I don't have any cash." Daniel said lifting his hands, "I only use cards."

The man became annoyed. It was obvious he'd never done this before and was desperate. "Just give me whatever you got. Your wallet. Your phone. Give me your jacket."

But Sora wasn't giving in. She just stared the man down. When the mugger noticed her colorful skin, he took a step back and aimed his knife at her. "Keep the fuck away from me, you scorpion cunt. Throw me your purse. If you come near me I'll cut your fucking throat."

Sora didn't say a word. She just sucked a mouthful of poison from her cheek and spit the venom in the man's face. His mouth dropped open in shock, confused about what just happened to him. But when the poison dripped into his eyes he screamed and dropped to the ground, trying to wipe the thick green venom from his face.

"Come on," Sora told Daniel, calmly taking him by the wrist and walking quickly past the screaming junkie.

"You bitch! You fucking bitch!" The man cried, more frightened than angry.

When they were a safe distance away, Sora turned back and said, "If you don't want to go blind you better rinse the poison from your eyes. You have less than a minute."

The man screamed and pulled himself to his feet, running through traffic to get to the café across the street, barely able to see anything in front of him. He yelled, "Fucking freak! I'm going to fucking kill you! Ugly bitch!"

But he came across as more pathetic than threatening. Sora didn't stop, leading them around the corner to safety.

"Holy shit," Daniel said.

He had no idea that scorpions had the ability to spit poison. It was one of the most badass things he'd ever seen.

When they got back to Sora's place, she slammed the door behind Daniel and lunged at him. She grabbed him around the waist and pulled him close to her, using her other hand to peel off his bomber jacket.

As she opened her mouth to kiss him, Daniel pulled away and wriggled out of her grip. She didn't stop taking off his coat and forced herself closer to him.

"What's wrong?" she asked, bringing her lips to his ear. "Aren't you turned on after that?"

Daniel panicked. He held out his hand between them. "I can't kiss you. You still have poison in your mouth."

She shook her head. "It's fine. I already swallowed it."

Daniel didn't move. He didn't believe her.

Sora picked up a bottle of bourbon on her coffee table and took a swig. Then she opened her mouth and stuck out her tongue. "It's all gone. Perfectly safe. I promise."

He still didn't feel comfortable kissing her.

She groaned in frustration, stepping closer. "Fine. We don't have to kiss on the mouth."

She pulled him close, her lips pressing against his neck, sucking on his throat like a vampire as she unzipped his pants.

Daniel's entire body tensed, his nerves screaming with a mix of fear and confusion. She felt dangerous, like she was a coiled rattlesnake ready to strike. But despite his fear, he found himself becoming erect. Maybe it was the alcohol dulling his instincts, but he leaned in, pressing his lips to her ruby-red neck. Her skin was unnervingly smooth and firm. It felt so alien and strange to him, like the skin of a frog's belly. He pushed his tongue against her neck and then pulled it back right away. Even though he knew that scorpions don't sweat poison from their skin, he still became worried that kissing her neck could somehow be dangerous.

But when Sora got his pants down and wrapped her fingers around his penis, he stopped worrying about her neck and started worrying about what was coming next.

"Don't..." he whispered, trying to step back. But she didn't release her grip around his penis.

She said, "It's fine. Don't worry about it."

He cringed and said, "I can't do it."

"Don't be such a pussy," she said. "I won't hurt you."

"I don't think I'm ready to have sex."

She sneered at him and her tone went from sensual to pissed off. "I just fucking saved your life back there. Are you really going to be an asshole now?"

Daniel took a deep breath and said, "I'm sorry..."

She grabbed his hand and shoved it into her pants. "Just finger me then."

Daniel didn't argue any further. She continued stroking his penis as she took her pants off. They masturbated each other while standing in her messy living room, grunting and groaning. As Daniel rubbed her clitoris, he tried to convince himself that it was safe. Intellectually he knew that he couldn't be poisoned by getting any of it on his fingers.

Once she was wet enough, Sora guided his fingers deeper

inside of her and moaned. Her insides felt unusual. Lumpier and fleshier than a normal woman's. The vaginal fluid was thicker, more like a jelly than a liquid. Daniel imagined that he could feel her poison glands within her. He imagined that the jelly-like fluid was her poison, covering his fingers. As soon as she released his hand, he removed his fingers and focused on her clitoris again. It terrified him but he didn't stop. He just suffered through it until he ejaculated all over his thighs and she came against his fingertips.

The whole experience was awkward and disturbing for him. When it was over, he pulled up his pants and ran to the bathroom to wash his hand off, trying to clean away every drop of her vaginal fluids just in case there was any poison mixed in.

When he returned to the living room, Sora was lying on the couch in her panties and t-shirt, drinking from the bottle of bourbon. He went over to the couch and sat down next to her. He didn't drink from the same bottle as her when she offered him a swig.

"Want to play some video games?" she asked him.

"Sure," he said.

She pulled out two Playstation controllers and they spent the rest of the night playing Overcooked and Borderlands and pretending that the awkward sexual experience they just had never happened.

CHAPTER
TWO

Sora and Daniel have been dating for a few months now, but they haven't been too serious with their relationship. They haven't had sex yet, outside of a few releases of sexual frustration that would leave them feeling gross and violated. But they've been enjoying going out and spending time at each other's places. They've even started sleeping over at each other's apartments from time to time. Daniel is getting much more comfortable with the idea of dating a scorpion. He's able to hug her and snuggle with her on the couch without worrying about being poisoned. But he avoids kissing her and is opposed to having sex.

Daniel can tell that she's losing patience with him. She wants a more intimate relationship. In fact, sex is probably one of the main things she's after in their relationship. They don't connect well as a couple. They are far from soul mates. They just both want to be in a relationship with someone, anyone, and haven't found a person better than each other. If a better prospect were to come along their relationship would be over in a heartbeat. But they've stayed together long enough that they have settled into a relationship. It just hasn't been a very intimate one.

Daniel realizes that he has to either build up the courage to sleep with her or call off their relationship. She tells him that it's all up to how much he trusts her. During sex, she has the power to kill him if she wants to. His hesitation is based on whether he believes she will use that power or not. She has tried to convince him that she is not dangerous, not a threat, and that she would never purposely poison him, but just the fact that she could kill him if she wants to is terrifying to Daniel. He can't think of any reason she'd want to kill him, but he still doesn't know much about her. She could be a complete psychopath for all he knows. And because of his experiences with past relationships, he has a hard time trusting women.

But he knows that she's not going to let him get away with wimping out for much longer. He has to have the guts to put his life in her hands if he doesn't want to go back to being single again. He realizes that being alone is the far worse option. He doesn't have to stay with her forever. He doesn't have to marry her or anything. But he does have to get over his fear, get over his trust issues, in order to keep their relationship going.

The night they plan to have sex, Daniel is freaking the fuck out. He can't believe he's actually going through with it. They discussed what kind of birth control they'd use. Daniel wanted to use condoms, hoping that the layer of latex would protect him from the poison, but Sora didn't want to. She said that her poison has a corrosive effect that would bleed through latex, so it wouldn't keep him safe if that's why he wanted to use them. The only defense from her venom is for the scorpion to have total control of her poison gland, which she says is second nature to her now. Daniel decides he has to believe her. They go with the pill instead.

Daniel has never seen Sora completely naked. He's seen parts of her before, in dim lighting. He's felt every inch of her body, but he's never seen her standing before him, exposing the full color of her aposematic body.

Her abdomen is bright sapphire blue from her crotch up to her chest. Her nipples are darker blue than her breasts and her belly is lighter than the rest of her body. Her thighs and crotch are a deep red color, darker than her face. And unlike her jet black hair, the hair on her body is a mixture of blue, red and yellow, depending on the color of skin beneath it.

Despite how alien she looks to Daniel, he can't help but see her as beautiful. He's not sure if he was completely attracted to her before. He found her sexy, but not necessarily pretty. But right now, in this moment, she might just be the most attractive woman he's ever been with. It's probably caused by his hormones due to not being with any other woman for so long. He's completely turned on by her right now. It almost helps relieve some of the fear.

"Are you sure you're ready for this?" she asks, rubbing her crotch at him.

He nods his head. "Yes."

"Good," she says, coming toward him. "Because I want you to be fearless tonight. I want you to go for it even if you think it will kill you."

Daniel gulps. For second, he thinks she just admitted that she plans to fuck him to death.

She crawls onto the bed with him and rubs her long black fingernails against his naked body. She goes right up to his face, staring him in the eyes.

"Show me how fearless you are," she says. "Kiss me."

Daniel leans forward and kisses her. He closes his eyes as she wraps her black lips around his and puts her tongue into his mouth. They kiss for only a minute until Sora is satisfied that he's not holding back. Then she lies down on the bed and spreads her legs.

"Now give me oral sex," she says.

"What?" Daniel asks. He didn't realize she wanted him to do that tonight.

"You're not scared of my pussy, are you?" she asks.

Even though he definitely is, he realizes that she's just testing him. She wants to see if he's finally willing to trust that she won't poison him while they are intimate.

But he still hesitates. When she sees the cautious look on his face, she says, "You're name's Daniel Munch. With a name like that, it's pretty much mandatory that you munch carpet."

Daniel groans when she says *munch carpet*. "That's so lame. I can't believe you said that."

There has been no shortage of people making that reference to his last name. Friends, girlfriends and childhood bullies have teased him about it his whole life. He can't believe even a scorpion would give him a hard time about it.

Sora laughs. "Come on. The last guy I fell in love with refused to do it. Show me you're better than him."

Daniel knows that kissing her and giving her oral sex are equally as dangerous and he's already survived kissing her, so he decides to go through with it. He wraps his arms around her thighs and buries his face in her bright blue pubic hair and lets go of his fears. She moans out loud before he even licks her and wraps her legs around his neck.

"Oh fuck!" she cries as he begins, grinding his head into her crotch. "Don't hold back."

Daniel tries not to hold back, but it's so alien to him. Her labia are salty and rubbery in his mouth, like sucking on live razor clams, and her flavor is unlike any woman he tasted before. He imagined it would be spicy, maybe because of the poison or her red chili pepper-colored skin, but it's sweet and mushroomy, like a mix of honey and truffle oil. The jelly-textured fluid coats his tongue and lips. If the substance is poison then he's already dead, so he fearlessly continues, accepting his fate.

When she's satisfied with his bravery, Sora sits up and crawls on top of him, pushing him firmly against the mattress. She guides his penis inside of her and drops all of her weight onto him.

"Shit yes!" she yells as she finds the right angle. "It's about fucking time!"

As she fucks him as hard as she can, Daniel realizes just how desperate she's been to get laid. She doesn't even look him in the eyes as she rides him, just happy to release all the sexual energy she had pent up inside her for so long. She doesn't even care who she's with. All she's been looking for is somebody who would give in and let her fuck them without fear of dying. Somebody she could be intimate with who wasn't an absolute psycho.

After her first orgasm, she laughs out loud and kisses Daniel all over his terrified face. Then she looks him in the eyes.

"Come on, Daniel," she says in a mischievous tone. "If you don't come I'm going to poison you."

When she says that, he tenses up but he doesn't lose his erection.

She finds it funny to see him squirm beneath her. "I'm serious. You better get into it if you don't want to die."

Teasing him starts to turn her on even more. She slows down a little, putting more effort into each thrust, leaning close to his ear, "You don't think I'll get away with it? I have your life in my hands and you know it."

Daniel panics. He struggles to get free, but she holds him in place. She fucks him until he comes inside of her. His pulsating member sends her into orgasm and she cries out loud, drooling against his chest. When they finish, he pulls himself out of her and pushes her away.

"What the fuck!" he yells. "What the fuck is wrong with you?"

She laughs at him. "I was just kidding. You were so stiff I had to break up the tension."

"But you said you were going to poison me…"

"I was just testing you," she says. "You said you would be fearless. I wanted to see how far I could go before you cracked."

Daniel inches away. "It wasn't funny."

She wraps her naked body around him and pulls him closer, laying her head on his chest. "Don't be such a wimp. It was fun."

Feeling her warmth against his skin, he loosens up a bit. He adjusts his position to get more comfortable and puts his arms around her.

She kisses him on the neck and says, "Thanks. I really needed that."

Then she tightens her grip on him and falls asleep. Daniel lies there, staring at the ceiling as she coils around him like a snake.

After that night, their relationship becomes all about sex. They stop going on dates with each other and just meet up at each other's apartments with beers and food four or five nights a week. Sora stays at his place most weekends and he spends the night at hers one or two nights during the week. Every time they become intimate, Daniel loses a little bit of his fear for her. He no longer believes that she would purposely poison him. And even though he still feels that he could be poisoned by accident, the risk seems to get less and less likely until he finally feels completely safe with her. Despite her inhuman skin, she is no different than any other girl he's dated. In fact, she is actually the most normal person he's ever been in a relationship with.

Love is the only part of their relationship that is missing. His friends and family all think he's insane for dating a scorpion and have been encouraging him to leave her. He hasn't seen any of them since he moved across country for work, so their opinions don't matter to him. He knows they wouldn't like her even if she wasn't a scorpion, especially since she used to be a cam girl, so he doesn't plan on introducing them to her even if their relationship gets more serious. But he wonders how long they will stay together. He doesn't want to spend the rest of his life with her or anything, but he doesn't want the relationship to end either. He assumes that someday the sex will get boring and they'll move on, but after a year of being together nothing has changed. Sora spends more time at his place than her own and out of nowhere he realizes that she's been waking up in bed with him for three weeks in a row. It seems stupid paying rent on two apartments so he agrees to let her move in.

Now his apartment is cluttered with mangas and empty beer cans and half-eaten bowls of cereal. Sora is probably the biggest slob of any girl he's ever dated. She owns so many outfits that she leaves scattered across every inch of his apartment. She has taken over his home and he doesn't even recognize it as his anymore. But there's no going back now. He agreed to let her move in and now he's stuck with her.

Daniel adapts to living with Sora after a few months. He spends most of his time in his guest room which he transformed into a home office. It is the only sanctuary he has left. Sora has claimed the rest of the apartment for her own, especially the living room where she spends most of her time, hanging out on the couch while drinking blush wine and playing video games or reading comics. She has three full-time jobs that she works remotely, putting in less than an hour of work on each per day, using AI assistants to do most of the work for her. She's obviously conning her employers and trying to get the most money while doing the least work possible. It won't be long before they find out and fire her, but she's milking them for all she can in the meantime and saving up as much money as possible for when that day comes.

Daniel now feels completely at ease with his girlfriend. He trusts that she is fully capable of controlling her poison and that he isn't in any danger. She could still kill him if she wanted to, but not any easier than any other woman could. Any girlfriend he's ever had could have stabbed him to death in his sleep, yet he wasn't afraid of that ever happening. It took him a while, but he eventually realized he wasn't in any danger around Sora.

The only time her venom was ever an issue was when she released a large quantity of it while taking a shower. Every once in a while, scorpions have to release the venom from their glands to prevent infection and retain potency. When she oozed the poison out of her vaginal gland, the poison evaporated in the hot shower and mixed with the steam. A toxic cloud filled the apartment, and though it wasn't deadly, it made Daniel sick for days. He had a massive headache and chills and his muscles ached. They put fans in all the windows and aired out the place, but it was a miserable experience for Daniel. He made her promise not to do that when he's home ever again.

Another problem with having Sora in his apartment is the looks he gets from his neighbors. Everyone used to be so nice to him and talk to him after they got off work or watch out for his Amazon packages so nobody would steal them. But now they all ignore him. They think he's a horrible person for dating a scorpion and are pissed that he would bring such a monster into their community. They hide their children whenever Sora comes up the stairs. They give both of them dirty looks and try to make it perfectly clear that she's not wanted here. Daniel is annoyed that they would be so judgmental, but he gets over it quickly. He'd rather be in a relationship with Sora and have everyone hate him than be alone. If his neighbors don't like it then they can just move out.

For the most part, Daniel likes having Sora around. She is pretty easygoing compared to his past girlfriends. He doesn't know how to say no to her, so she pretty much gets her way whenever she wants something, but she doesn't ever ask for anything too unreasonable. She gets to choose what they eat for dinner or what movie they watch or what side of the bed she sleeps on or when they have sex. She also has no problem leaving the house a mess so it's usually up to Daniel to keep the place clean. She never does the dishes. She won't even go to the store and so he has to do all the shopping.

There are a few times when Daniel thinks she goes too far with her domineering behavior. When he goes to the bathroom, she will often bang on the door and tell him to get off the toilet because she has to take a shit. The first time he refused she entered the bathroom anyway and relieved herself in the bathtub. It was so disgusting to clean up that Daniel never refused her again. He'd rather hold his bowels and hand over the toilet than have to clean up his girlfriend's shit. She also kicks him out of their bed if he's snoring or if she wants to spread out. Sometimes she stays up late at night and blasts anime so loud that he needs to wear earplugs.

But on his birthday, Sora went all out. She surprised him with plane tickets to Tokyo, a place they both always wanted to visit. Even though the timing was too short notice with his job and he had to pull a lot of strings in order to get time off work, most of it unpaid, he was still able to go on a crazy adventure with his girlfriend that he never expected he'd ever be able to do in his life. He had no idea she cared about him so much to give him such an amazing present.

In their hotel room in Tokyo, Sora asks a question Daniel wasn't expecting.

Lying on the bed and flipping through her phone to figure out what they should do the next day, Sora asks, "Should we get married?"

Daniel nearly trips over his pants on the way to brush his teeth.

"What?" he asks, a shocked expression on his face.

"I was just thinking about it," she says, not looking up from her phone. "We've been together longer than anyone else I've ever dated. It seems to be going fine. I don't see any reason to break up with you, so I was just wondering how far we should take this thing."

Daniel can't believe she would mention marriage. They aren't even that close of a couple.

"Are you saying you *want* to marry me?" Daniel asks.

She shrugs. "I'm not against considering it. This isn't a proposal or anything, I just wanted to know what you think about marriage."

"I would like to get married someday, to somebody."

"But not to me?"

"I didn't say that."

"So you would want to marry me?"

Daniel hesitated, "I'm not sure. Would you want to marry me?"

"Sure. If you proposed to me right now I would probably say yes."

"Probably?"

"Well, I'd have some conditions. But if you agreed to them, I'd definitely say yes."

Daniel sits down. His heart is racing with worry. She's never even told him that she loves him. He can't believe that she'd skip that part of their relationship and jump straight to marriage. This is all too sudden for him. She hasn't even looked up from her phone for a second during this conversation.

"Like what?" he asks.

"Well, I made a promise to myself to never marry a man unless he was willing to do the switch with me."

"You want to switch bodies?"

She nods her head. "For a month, just enough time for you to see what it's like to live as me, to really understand what it means to be a scorpion. And I'd get to see what it's like to be you."

"But body swapping is an expensive procedure," Daniel says. "I can't afford that."

She waves off his concern. "I'll pay for it. I have plenty of money saved up. It'll be fine." She puts her phone down and turns off the light by her side of the bed. "I'll make the appointment when we get back home."

As she rolls over and goes to sleep, Daniel just sits there in silence. He doesn't remember agreeing to do the body switching procedure. He didn't even agree to marry her. But that's just the kind of person Sora is. She always makes decisions like this for the both of them without finishing a conversation. If he didn't want to marry her, pretty much the only answer he could possibly give her was no. Anything else she would take as a yes.

CHAPTER
THREE

When they get back from Japan, Sora books an appointment with a body swapping service before Daniel tells her that he's not ready for such a procedure. He tries wiggling out of it without telling her directly that he doesn't want to do the switch with her.

"How am I going to go to work if I'm in your body?" he asks.

She doesn't look up, flipping through an erotic art book she bought in Tokyo. "Just tell your employer you're doing the switch tomorrow. People switch bodies all the time these days. They'll understand I'm sure. I work from home so I'll be fine doing my work in your body."

Daniel doesn't know how else to argue with her. Body swapping technology has become really popular in recent years. A lot of celebrities have been promoting it, especially actors who can switch bodies with people temporarily in order to play different kinds of roles. It has been a godsend for the transgender community and attractive people who are willing to trade their good looks for large quantities of money. But it has been especially popular among young couples who are considering marriage.

The new trend is for couples to switch bodies in order to see the world from each other's perspective. It makes them grow closer and have a deeper understanding for one another. But it is usually out of reach to everyone but the richest of couples.

Daniel never expected that he'd ever have to go through with it. He can't imagine what it will be like to live as a woman for a whole month, let alone a venomous woman. He has no idea what he's getting himself into.

Sora drives them to the place where they are to get the operation, but the place isn't what Daniel expected. It's an old abandoned warehouse that used to belong to a trucking company that went out of business years ago.

Daniel looks around, confused, when they get out of the car. "Where are we? This isn't the hospital."

"We're not going through the hospital," she says. "They charge way too much."

"What? I thought you said you could afford it."

She shakes her head. "Not at full price. This guy charges a tenth as much for the same procedure. He cuts out the taxes and all the money the hospital would take. We only have to pay the doctor and he makes the same amount as he normally would."

"Is it safe?"

"Of course it is. I wouldn't do it if it wasn't safe. He's a real doctor. He does these procedures all the time. He just offers these services on the side for poor people who can't afford it. He doesn't think this operation should be reserved only for rich people."

Daniel is much more nervous than he was before. He doesn't know if he wants to switch bodies with Sora. He doesn't even know if he wants to marry her. But doing the procedure illegally by some strange doctor who might not have any real qualifications fills Daniel with so much dread that he can barely walk straight.

They are let into the building at a side entrance, a doctor's assistant checking Sora's identification and leading them into the back. She pays upfront, in all cash. Daniel doesn't know how much it is but it could easily be twenty or thirty thousand dollars. That's a lot of money to throw at a test of their relationship. Daniel had no idea she was that serious about their future together.

"Are you sure you want to pay that much for this?" Daniel asks while they stand in a decaying unfurnished back room, waiting for the doctor to be ready for them. "That much money could go toward a down payment on a house."

"I'd rather spend a lot of money on this than on a big wedding. If it doesn't work out then we'll know we don't belong together. I'd rather lose a bunch of money now than waste years of my life on a bad marriage."

"And you're sure you want to marry me if this works out?"

"Of course I am. I'm not going to wait around for the perfect man to come along. I want to get married by the time I turn thirty and you check all the right boxes for me. This test is all that's left for me to make a final decision on whether we're right for each other."

Daniel nods. His hands are visibly shaking. He wonders if he's really able to go through with the procedure. At this point, Sora's already paid a lot of money so there's no way to back out without dumping her on the spot. She would be so pissed at him and rightfully so. He's had bad experiences with vengeful ex-girlfriends, but dumping a woman after she's put up thousands of dollars to strengthen their relationship would be something that would bring out a wrath worse than anything he's ever experienced before. The fact that she's a scorpion only makes the idea all the more terrifying.

He knows he has to go for it, at least with the switch. Marriage on the other hand is a different story. He doesn't despise the idea of marrying Sora. Perhaps if they were married the relationship would get better. Perhaps they would actually fall deeply in love with each other. Friendship comes first. That's what his mother always said. And he definitely sees Sora as a great friend. He thinks it's possible for their relationship to work out eventually. The big hurdle to get over will be telling his friends and family that he's marrying the scorpion girl he's been dating.

When the doctor comes to get them, he doesn't say much. He has his face covered to hide his identity. No name tag. Just a middle-aged white guy with glasses and purple contacts. If anything goes wrong, they won't know who to blame. The police won't be able to do anything about it.

They are taken into a large room with no windows. The operating area seems to have been set up only hours ago. Two wheeled stretchers like those from an ambulance are standing side-by-side near some large equipment that Daniel doesn't recognize.

"Lie down on these," the doctor says in a low tone of voice, pointing to the gurneys.

Sora and Daniel climb onto the makeshift beds as the doctor's assistant straps them down. Their heads are placed in a bowl-shaped device with tubes and wires connected to the machine behind them. The assistant puts ventilators over their mouths and begins to apply the anesthesia.

Daniel panics. Fear floods his system, suddenly realizing what a crazy thing he's doing right now. He can't go through with it. He can't switch bodies with another person even if it is somebody he was truly in love with. He fights against the straps, yelling at them to stop the procedure.

But his muscles relax as the anesthetic takes effect. He goes limp and his eyes roll back as his consciousness fades.

Daniel regains some consciousness an hour later. His mind is foggy and he can barely focus on anything. Someone assists him to another room and lays him down on a cot and he goes back to sleep.

It takes time before enough of the anesthetic leaves his system for him to regain consciousness. When he wakes up, he wonders if the procedure is complete. He sits up and feels a pain in the back of his head. When he lifts his arm to feel the bandage on his scalp, he notices the blue skin tone of his arm. He looks down and sees that he's wearing Sora's clothes. He's inside of her body.

"What the fuck?" he says in a woman's voice.

His voice doesn't sound like his but it doesn't sound like Sora's either. It's softer and strangely more feminine. He also doesn't have Sora's Tennessee accent.

"Oh my god…"

The room is empty. No sign of Sora or the doctors. He tries to stand up but his legs are weak. His mind is still a little foggy. As he takes a few steps, he realizes that he has trouble with balance. He's not sure if it's because there's still some anesthesia in his body or because he's not accustomed to using somebody else's legs to walk.

The feeling of being in Sora's skin is strange. When he touches his arm, the sensation is foreign to him. Her aposematic skin is so smooth to the touch. It feels like he is touching Sora's arm despite it now being his own arm. His breasts are bigger and heavier than he was expecting. He always thought of her breasts as average in size, but as someone who's used to having no breasts at all they now feel way too big. The bra straps are tight and itchy against his ribcage. He doesn't know if he should touch them without Sora's permission, so he keeps his hands away from them for now, even though he wants to push them up higher to be more comfortable in the painful bra.

But despite feeling awkward with the boobs on his chest, the sensation in his underwear is actually a relief. It was always difficult to find a comfortable place for his penis. Despite having a much larger than average penis, Daniel was never happy with how uncomfortable it was having a member that size. It would also fall through the leg of his underwear or get stuck to the side of his leg whenever he was sweaty. He had to adjust it all the time. Formfitting pants were never an option. If his penis gets too squished in a pair of tight jeans it would bother him all day long. But in Sora's body, his crotch feels like it has so much space. Though at this moment he really doesn't want to think about how he has a vagina instead of a penis. That thought is far too strange for him. He really doesn't know what to think about having his genitals changed like this. It's going to take a while to get used to it.

Daniel steps out of the room and sees his own body speaking to the doctor at the end of the hallway. It's surreal seeing himself. And for some reason, his body looks so much different now. It's not like looking in a mirror or seeing a video of yourself. In fact, it's difficult to even see his body as himself. There's a definite resemblance, but it's more like running into someone with striking similarities to yourself than seeing a mirror image.

They say that mirrors and videos don't really capture what a person looks like in real life. Perhaps what he is seeing now is what he really looks like to everyone else. Or perhaps his physical appearance has somehow changed now that Sora is in his body. The way she holds herself is so much different than he does. Her facial expressions aren't the same. She even seems more masculine than he has ever felt in his own skin.

When Daniel gets to Sora, the doctor says his goodbyes and disappears. Sora turns to him and says, "There you are. How do you feel?"

Her voice is different from Daniel's. She has the Tennessee accent that she did in her own body, but she speaks in a stronger and more masculine tone. She also seems more comfortable in his skin than he's ever felt in it before.

"Strange." His voice is still coming out soft and meek. "Very strange."

She nods. "I know, right?" She grips his shoulder. "Come on. We've got to clear out of here as soon as we can. Are you okay to walk?"

He nods. "I think so."

She wraps her arm around his shoulder and helps guide him out of the warehouse and back to the car. It feels so awkward to feel his own arm wrapped around him. His body seems so much taller than he thought he was.

"Let's go home," she says from the driver's seat, starting up the car.

They head back to the apartment. Daniel sits uneasily in his seat, not sure how to get comfortable in his new body. He doesn't know if he's ready to start his life as his own girlfriend.

As the initial shock of the procedure wears off, Daniel realizes just how strange it is to be in somebody else's body. It's not just the smooth texture of her skin that is odd and alien to him. His eyes are different as well. Colors aren't the same when looking through Sora's eyes. Everything appears a little different. Reds are brighter but blues are duller. Greens look a little more yellowish and orange looks a little more reddish. He had heard that people see colors differently based on genetics and the structure of their eyes, but he had no idea the difference was so dramatic.

But every moment exploring his familiar world in Sora's body, Daniel finds new divergences.

Sora is shorter than Daniel by quite a bit, so seeing his apartment from a lower perspective is new and kind of awkward, but also a bit more useful. He doesn't have to watch his head near the shelves in his office. His desk chair is roomier and more comfortable. Though now he can't reach books on the top of his bookcase or control the volume without a remote on his ceiling-mounted television.

His hands are also softer and smaller than he's used to, making controlling simple things like pens and forks more difficult. Daniel was left-handed and because Sora is right-handed she hasn't built up the proper muscles in her left hand for him to use it very well. So doing anything with Sora's left hand is difficult to accomplish. She also has long fingernails that she tells him he's not allowed to cut and has to be careful not to break them, which makes using his hands even more difficult.

This is something Daniel is not going to enjoy about the next month, but there are things he is very happy about. Sora is in much better shape than Daniel, so being in her body gives him more energy than he normally would have. He doesn't have the same urge to sit down and relax as he did in his own body. He can stay on his feet longer, move around without getting tired. He's lighter on his feet, far more flexible, and just generally feels better physically and emotionally than he did before.

But Sora has really bad seasonal allergies and her nasal passage is more narrow than Daniel's. With his sinuses constantly clogged, he has to breathe only through his mouth or blow his nose every five minutes. He didn't realize just how annoying allergies were for people who have them but it's enough to drive him insane.

At dinner, Daniel is shocked to discover how different things taste with Sora's tongue. They ordered Thai food and Daniel got his second favorite dish, green curry with chicken. He couldn't get his favorite, crab fried rice, because Sora is allergic to shellfish. But he usually loves green curry just as much, especially from the place across the street, but it tastes so weird and funky. The flavors are so much different. Kind of earthy and tart.

"I don't like this," he tells Sora, slowly chewing an unpleasant bite.

Sora nods. "Thai curry is disgusting. It's got coconut in it. I hate coconut."

Daniel pushes the plate across the table. "Taste it. Is it off or is it just me?"

Despite being suspicious, Sora takes a bite. Her eyes light up. "Holy shit. That's delicious."

She pulls the plate away from him and starts shoveling the curry in her mouth.

"How is this so good?" she says with her cheeks full. "I fucking love it."

"I kind of hate it."

She passes her pad prik king—green bean stir fry with beef—over to him and says, "Try mine."

He takes a bite and nods his head. "I like it better but it still tastes weird."

Sora takes huge spoonfuls of both dishes and piles it onto her plate. "I have such a huge appetite in your body. I love it."

Daniel eats a few more bites before he is full and pushes his plate away. He doesn't have much of an appetite for some reason.

Sora says, "Being a man is kind of awesome. I can eat all I want and don't have to worry about gaining weight."

"Men gain weight just as much as women," Daniel argues.

She shakes her head. "It's not the same." Then she looks over at him and points her fork in his direction. "Don't you dare make me fat when you're in my body. I'll fucking kill you."

"Don't make me fat either," Daniel says. "You're eating way more than I would."

She shrugs and keeps eating.

It's weird for Daniel to sit at a table, watching Sora control his body. Just the way she eats is different than he would eat. The way her lips move, the way she sits in her chair. In some ways it seems like he's hanging out with some weird guy he's never met before and in other ways it feels like he's interacting with himself from a different body. He wonders if this is what it would be like if you had a long lost identical twin and they entered your life for the first time while you were both in adulthood. He wonders if this is what it's like to have an out of body experience. But at the same time she still sounds like Sora, even though she is now a man. He can still tell it's her whenever she speaks. Even the way she sits in her chair. It's just surreal. It's especially odd how comfortable Sora seems in his body, like she's spent her whole life as him already. He doesn't think he'll ever feel that way being her. He doesn't think he'll ever be able to get used to this whatsoever.

They lie in bed together. Daniel is scrolling social media while Sora reads a volleyball-themed manga next to him.

"It's so great being able to read without my glasses," she says, turning the page with excitement. "You're lucky you have good eyes."

As she says this, Daniel realizes how difficult it has been for him to read the text on his phone.

"Yeah, I can hardly read a thing," he says, squinting his eyes.

Sora takes the reading glasses from the nightstand on her side of the bed and hands them to him. "Try these."

When Daniel puts them on, he realizes he can read the text on his phone better but not as good as he could in his old body. There's a glare on his glasses that makes it difficult to see. The glasses are also scratched up and dirty. He has no idea how Sora's been able to read with these things for so long.

When she's ready to go to bed, Sora turns off the light and rolls over, snuggling up to Daniel. He tenses up, feeling awkward having his own arm wrapped around him. She rubs his shoulder and presses her face against his neck. Her skin is hot and unpleasant against him. He heard that men have warmer body temperatures than women, but he didn't realize how much. He feels smothered by her warmth and squirms to get away. As someone who loves the cold, he doesn't like being so close to her even if she wasn't in his own skin.

This is the part of the night when they usually have sex. Sora has always been pretty determined that they have sex every single night at the end of every single day as long as she's not sick or on her period. In fact, their sex life is the main reason they have been together for so long. Despite not having much in common, they've been able to connect intimately ever since Daniel was able to get over the venomous nature of her as a scorpion.

Daniel assumed they would put their love life on hold while they were in each other's bodies, but when Sora's penis gets hard and he feels it rubbing against his hip, Daniel begins to panic.

"I don't think I'm going to be able to have sex with you while you're in my body," Daniel tells her.

Sora stops grinding against him and laughs. "Yeah, I know what you mean. Sleeping with myself would be weird." She rolls over on her back, staring up at the ceiling. "But we've got to try it. At least once."

Daniel wraps his arms around his lower abdomen, almost

to protect himself. "I don't know…"

Sora says, "We've got a whole month. We don't have to rush into it."

But Daniel really hates the idea. Even though Sora has had romantic experiences with women in the past and probably wouldn't find it as strange, he has absolutely no interest in making love to a man in a woman's body. And even if he did, the idea of making love to his own body is even worse. He is disgusted by his own body. Even among other men, he finds himself repulsive. Sora isn't the same. She has always found herself attractive. She's a bit of a narcissist in fact. Despite spending most of her time lounging on the couch playing video games, she still makes a point to exercise every day and stay in shape because she likes feeling attractive. She finds herself to be one of the most beautiful women in the world. She probably wouldn't have a problem having sex with herself. But Daniel never could in a million years.

"We can at least masturbate, can't we?" Sora asks.

Although the lights are off, Daniel can tell Sora is already rubbing her erect penis.

"It feels so cool," she says, pulling off her underwear and grabbing her dick tighter. "Holy shit…"

Daniel just sits there in silence as his fiancé indulges in his body, rubbing her manly chest and stroking her penis. She jerks herself off until she comes all over the bed sheets, giggling and squealing with childish enthusiasm.

When she finishes, she rubs her dick off on the comforter and then rolls over and grips Daniel tightly.

"That was so fucking fun," she says. "You have to try it."

Daniel just lies there, feeling awkward. "Maybe another time."

"It's so different cumming as a guy," she says. "I'm going to jerk off so much in your body."

He can feel her smiling against his cheek.

"I'll let you borrow my vibrator," she says. "You need to see what it's like to cum as a woman."

Daniel feels awkward discussing it. "I don't know…"

"No, I mean… you have to. Part of the reason I wanted us to switch bodies is so that you'll understand how to please me in bed. I want you to masturbate in me as much as you can. Then you'll know what gets me off."

Daniel just nods his head. As turned on as he is by the idea of masturbating in a woman's body, he's still afraid of his own vagina due to the venom glands. He worries that he might get poison on his fingers and kill someone with it. If he killed Sora while she's in his body then he would not only lose her, but he'd also never be able to return to his own body ever again.

It will take quite a bit of time before he'll feel comfortable masturbating in Sora's body.

CHAPTER
FOUR

In the morning, Daniel wakes up with the weight of Sora's hot and sweaty man arm wrapped around him, hugging him between his breasts. He pushes her off of him and climbs out of bed, his bladder full and dying to be released. He rushes to the bathroom and drops down on the toilet, falling into the bowl, his butt dipping into the icy cold toilet water. When Sora moved in, he made sure to keep the toilet seat down for her sake, knowing how much she would be annoyed with it. But now that she's a man, she doesn't pay him the same respect. She must have been so excited to be able to pee standing up that she didn't think about putting the seat back down. Either that or she was getting revenge for every man who ever left the seat up for her in the past.

Daniel gets up and puts the seat down and then pees into the toilet. It's his first time peeing as a woman. Even though he had to go the day before, he felt too embarrassed to do it in Sora's body, especially while she was around him. But this morning, he doesn't have a choice. He has to go too bad.

Peeing as a woman is not at all what he expected. For some reason, he thought his urine stream would be much thicker. He thought it would just gush out of him since it doesn't have to be filtered through a fleshy tube. But it's actually much thinner and his urine stream doesn't have as much pressure as it did as a male. Not only that, but it gets all over him. He can feel the

51

urine touch his skin down there and he finds it very unpleasant.

Before he finishes, he realizes he also has to poop and lets it go. Unlike peeing, pooping is much more pleasant in Sora's body than he's used to. The poop is such a soft texture and comes out so easily. He doesn't even have to strain or put much effort into it. In his body, he usually had to force it out and it took way too much time even during the rare times that he wasn't constipated. But Sora has a much healthier diet and doesn't eat as much, so he has no problem with bowel movements. He didn't realize that going to the bathroom could be so quick and easy.

Before he wipes, he looks down at his crotch. It's the first time he's seen his pubic region since he entered Sora's body. Her bright blue pubic hair looks even more alien when he sees it between his legs. Before it seemed like it was just dyed blue artificially, but upon closer inspection he can see the roots. He can tell that it's natural.

When he wipes, he makes sure to move the wad of toilet paper from front to back. As a guy, he always went back to front, but he read that if women do that it could cause an infection. He never asked Sora about this so he's not sure if that's true, but he does it anyway just to be on the safe side.

As he wipes the toilet paper across his vulva, he starts to think about the poison glands inside of him. He doesn't know where they are located within him. He also doesn't know how to control them. Does he need to flex some kind of muscles inside of there to hold the poison in? Or does he need to use muscles in order to squeeze the poison out? He doesn't know. Since he's not used to having a vagina, he isn't sure what is normal and what is different between scorpions and normal women.

As he pulls up his underwear, he sees a period stain on the inside of his panties. It's almost tan in color and looks almost like a skid mark that he used to get as a guy when he didn't wipe his butt properly, though much lighter in color and in the wrong place. Daniel thinks there's no way that he can wear these underwear out in public, feeling embarrassed for some reason. Even though the stain is odorless, he thinks he needs to throw it away and buy new underwear for Sora while he's in her body.

"Don't fuck up any of my clothes," Sora tells Daniel as he tries to get dressed for work.

He never paid attention to what Sora wore, so he has difficulty traversing her wardrobe. She has a very messy system for organizing her clothes. Most of them are just in a pile in the corner of the living room. Others are piled high in the closet. She says she never wears any of the clothes in the closet so Daniel spends most of his morning digging through clothes to find something clean enough to wear. Since Sora works from home, she doesn't have any work clothes. All of her garments are either for comfort or style. Daniel has no idea what outfit she owns that would be passable for his business-casual-attire job.

Sora helps him pick out an outfit and dresses him, at least this once, since he seemed completely lost and helpless to her. When he looks at himself in the mirror, he thinks it still seems a little too casual. He's wearing brown pants and a sweater, but for some reason he still thinks it's way too sexy of an outfit to leave the house in. His boobs are so pronounced that they would have turned him on if he saw Sora wearing this outfit on a date.

"I hope it will work," Daniel says, as he stares at himself in the mirror and lets out a sigh from his ruby red lips.

When he gets to work, the male receptionist panics when he sees a scorpion enter the office building. The man is much younger than Daniel and is kind of a lazy self-absorbed gossip-junkie that he has always avoided.

"Can I help you?" the receptionist asks him in a nervous tone.

Daniel holds up his work ID even though it's a photo of his old body. "I'm Daniel Munch. I'm in accounting. I went through a body swap with my fiancé, so I don't look like myself right now."

The receptionist just stares at him for a moment, like he didn't hear a word he said.

Daniel adds, "Jim Davis, my boss, approved of it. He should have let you know."

As Daniel moves toward the receptionist to show him the approval letter, the man jumps back, not wanting a scorpion to come anywhere near him.

"Okay, fine," the receptionist cries, holding up his hands as though Daniel has a gun. "Do whatever you want, just stay away from me."

Daniel feels weird that the guy would react like that. He's worked in the same office with him for the last couple years and never knew he was such a racist.

"Okay..." Daniel says, walking away slowly toward the elevator.

Before he leaves the area, he hears the receptionist say, "Fucking scorpions..." And Daniel can't believe his ears. He almost wants to go back and confront him about what he said.

It's the first person he's interacted with after becoming Sora and he can't believe the experience was so unpleasant. Daniel assumes the guy is just an asshole. He never liked him anyway. But the second he gets to his floor, he realizes how differently everyone reacts to him. People he's worked with for years give him the dirtiest looks. People who have always been so nice to him are now looking at him with disgust, like they don't want his kind around. He had told them all that he was doing the switch with his fiancé, that he would be coming to the office as a woman, but he never mentioned what his fiancé looked like. They had no idea he was engaged to a scorpion. Even the women who were excited that he was doing the switch, who were so amused to see their coworker coming to work as a woman, seem appalled by him. It's like he's some kind of horrible pedophile that none of them want anything to do with.

And by the time he sits down at his desk and everyone realizes that the scorpion is really Daniel Munch, they get even more upset. They know that he will be in her body for a whole month and can't handle the idea of being around such a dangerous creature for that long. Many of them have had brothers, cousins, children and friends who have been poisoned by scorpions and so they hate them with a passion. They don't care that it's really Daniel in a scorpion's body. He's just as guilty for falling in love with such a repulsive freak of nature.

Daniel tries to tune everyone out and get some work done, but it's not so easy. Everyone has their eyes on him. People from other departments are coming to accounting just to see him wearing a scorpion's skin. They laugh and whisper about him behind his back, making audible cringing noises and expressing their revulsion without caring about his feelings.

He hears one guy from sales say, "What a fucking idiot. I'd never put my dick in a scorpion, let alone switch bodies with one."

The person he's talking to is surprisingly a woman. She says, "Oh, but he's pwobabwe in wuv wit her," in the most condescending baby voice possible.

They both laugh.

"Imagine what their kids will look like," the man says.

The woman says, "I would drown mine in the river if they came out looking like that."

Daniel doesn't react. He just stays in his seat, fuming mad, trying to focus on work. He doesn't personally know either of them, but he's pretty sure they are the biggest bullies in the office who are shitty to everyone even when they aren't scorpions.

But the people who really get to him are the people he thought were the nicest in the office. The two women who always used to talk to him every morning and tell him about their kids and their favorite Netflix shows now treat him like the worst person in the world. They hover around his workstation and one of them says, "Do you smell that? I went to school with a scorpion. They smell so gross."

The other one says, "Yeah, it's like dead frogs. Kind of fishy and rancid."

"Are we going to have to deal with this stench all month?"

"I hope not."

"I'm going to have to start wearing a facemask."

"We should complain…"

"God, she's so ugly."

"Poor Daniel."

"I thought he was smarter than that."

"He must have been desperate."

"Who the hell would be that desperate?"

"If my son came home with a scorpion I would have her arrested."

"I would disown mine."

"If I had to deal with smelly scorpion grandkids I would just die."

"They probably don't even have souls."

"Did you see that documentary on YouTube? It proved how they are related to demons. They were created by the devil to infect humanity."

"Poor Daniel. He's going to hell."

"Maybe we should try to save him."

"It's too late. He's already corrupted."

"Not necessarily."

"But he's surely already had sex with her. He's in her body. I bet he's going to reek like scorpion for the rest of his life."

"I thought I smelled something funny coming from him for a while now."

"Yeah. He was always kind of gross, wasn't he?"

"Yeah. He was always kind of a creep."

After a while of hearing this, Daniel gets fed up. He turns to them and says, "I can hear you."

The women just ignore him and go back to their desks.

One of them says, "She has such an ugly voice, too."

Daniel has never wanted to punch anyone more than he does now. Even though he always thought of them as friends, he had no idea how horrible they really were. He had no idea they were so racist. They are both white but one of them is married to a black man. The other adopted a Hispanic child. He expected better from them. But now he knows that deep down they are both assholes. And they feel justified to be assholes. Because scorpions sometimes kill young men, they assume that all venomous women are deserving of hate. They aren't the bad people, scorpions are. And bad people should all just go to hell and leave all of the honest good family-loving people alone.

Just after lunch, Daniel's boss calls him into his office. Jim Davis was always a pretty friendly guy. Compared to previous bosses he has had, Jim is nicer than average and usually lets him get away with whatever he wants. He'll let Daniel take days off whenever he needs them and leave early if he's got something else he needs to do. He's kind of a pushover in some ways. He doesn't have a whole lot of backbone. But today Jim doesn't seem like his normal self. As Daniel enters his office, he can see the look of absolute terror on his face.

"You wanted to see me, Jim?" Daniel asks.

His boss is obviously bothered by the sight of seeing a scorpion in his office. Just the sight of Daniel makes him cower in his seat.

Jim's voice trembles as he speaks. "Is that really you, Daniel? I didn't believe it when I heard."

"Of course it's me." Although hearing the feminine voice coming out of his mouth is foreign even to him.

Daniel goes to take a seat in front of Jim's desk, but Jim holds up his hands and yells, "Don't sit there!" Daniel pauses. "Is it okay if you just stand?"

Daniel backs off, confused about why it's so important that he doesn't sit down. But he quickly realizes that it's because Jim's worried that his venomous vagina might get poison all over the seat. It pisses him off quite a bit, but he decides not to react negatively.

Jim tries to calm down. He takes a deep breath and then asks, "What's going on, Daniel? Why are you in that body?"

"I told you before that I was going to do the switch with my fiancé. You approved of it weeks ago."

"Yeah, but you never said she was a scorpion."

"Does that matter? I never thought you of all people would be racist."

"I'm not racist!" Jim yells, then tries to calm down again. "I want that to be clear right now. I have no problem with people of other races, even scorpions. But having a venomous woman in the office is dangerous. I'm worried about everyone's safety."

"They aren't dangerous. *I'm* not dangerous."

"But I read on the internet that scorpions—"

Daniel cuts him off. "Don't believe any of those bullshit

stereotypes. I used to believe them myself. But once I started dating Sora, I realized that they're not true."

"Still, you *are* poisonous right now. You do have poison in your body that is strong enough to kill someone."

"But Charles in Collections is big enough to crush a person's skull with his bare hands. Just because he can kill someone doesn't mean that he will. He's not any more or less dangerous than I am."

Jim shakes his head. "It's not the same thing. Besides, the problem isn't whether you're dangerous or not. The problem is that you're being a disturbance in the office. Seven different people complained about you being here. Two of them threatened to quit if you didn't leave."

Daniel is shocked to hear this. "What? Are you serious? Who said that?"

Jim doesn't answer his question. "I can't have you working here while you're in that body. Can you switch back?"

Daniel shakes his head. "Not until the end of the month."

"Are you sure?"

Daniel thinks about it for a minute. He would really like to get back into his own body. He wonders if he can convince Sora to change back, using the excuse that his boss forced him to. But he knows how that will turn out. There's no way Sora would be cool with it. She would be pissed if he chose his job over her. He doesn't have a choice.

"I'm sorry, I can't," he tells his boss.

Jim sighs. "Well, you can't come to the office until you turn back. How much vacation time do you have left?"

"About a week."

"Well, you're going to have to take unpaid leave for the rest of the time."

"Can't I just work remotely?"

Jim shakes his head. "We don't do that anymore. I'm sorry, but my hands are tied."

Daniel panics. There's no way he can go three weeks

without pay. "Come on, Jim. I've worked here for years. Can't you make an exception this one time? You know I can do my job from home. I did it during the pandemic."

But his boss won't budge. He asks him to leave his office. When Daniel goes back to his desk, he finds himself surrounded by security. He has two minutes to get his stuff and leave.

*

On his way home, Daniel goes to the store to get some things Sora asked for. He has no idea how he's going to get by without pay for the month. He has a tiny amount of savings but he really didn't want to tap into it. He would ask Sora for help but she already emptied her bank account in order to pay for the body swap procedure. It's going to be a long difficult month. He wonders if he should just call off the engagement to get his body back. He's not even sure he wants to marry Sora. He doesn't want to be alone again, but it might be time he put some thought into how serious he actually is about the woman who now possesses his body.

At the store, he notices everyone staring at him. They all give him the evil eye, avoiding him when he pushes his cart down the aisle. Mothers hide their children behind their backs. Men turn around and walk the other way. Two college-aged guys notice him walking behind them and one of them says, "Look out. Death cunt on your six." Then they laugh.

He has to go through the self-checkout because every lane operated by an employee suddenly closes the second he gets in their line. And even in the self-checkout lane he is avoided by everyone. The employee doesn't come to assist him when he needs to have his ID checked for buying alcohol. The people in line behind him decide they'd rather stay in line than enter the area until he's finished and leaves.

Even after a single day as a scorpion, Daniel is beginning

to understand what Sora has had to deal with. He now knows why she wanted to do the switch in the first place. She's living in a completely different world than he is. There's no way that he could ever comprehend what it means to be a scorpion without living in her skin for a while. If he was in her shoes he would have done the same thing.

CHAPTER
FIVE

*

When he gets home, Daniel finds Sora masturbating in front of the bathroom mirror. She is naked and groping her body, using a dildo on her anus as she jerks off her penis, moaning loudly while locking eyes with herself in the mirror.

At first, Daniel is disturbed that she would be using his body in such a perverted manner without his permission. He feels violated. But he also thinks of it as kind of flattering. The way she stares at herself in Daniel's body, so turned on by his appearance, makes him blush. He had no idea that she was that physically attracted to him before. Even though he's not in his skin, it's like she's making love to him rather than herself. Being the object of her masturbation fantasy fills him with pride and confidence. He's never seen a woman so infatuated with his body before, especially one as beautiful as Sora.

She doesn't notice him as he watches her. She closes her eyes and leans her head back as she ejaculates into the bathroom sink. Then she lets out a sigh and washes off her penis and cleans the dildo that was in her ass.

When she turns to see Daniel watching her, she yelps and covers herself.

"What are you doing home so soon?" she cries, pulling up her boxer briefs.

"My boss sent me home early."

"What? Why?"

Sora gets dressed, pretending that nothing happened as Daniel explains what happened with his boss and coworkers. She is deeply annoyed by the story.

When he finishes, she tells him, "Fuck that place. Quit and get another job."

"I've had that job for years. I don't want to quit."

"Fuck that. I don't want you to work for a bunch of racist assholes. Get a better job."

Sora plops down on the couch and pulls out her game controller. She doesn't bring up the act that Daniel walked in on a few minutes ago, but he can't stop thinking about it. Although it was surreal to see her masturbating in his own body, he still feels mildly aroused by it.

Sora mentions it before he does. "How do men get anything done when they have a penis? I've masturbated three times today."

"I only masturbate once a week max," he says.

"No wonder why I'm so horny. You've got too much sexual energy pent up."

"How much do you normally masturbate? You know, when you're in your real body."

"More than once a week."

"I've never seen you masturbate before."

She shrugs. "I do it when you're at work."

"Oh…"

"You should try masturbating in my body." She tosses him the dildo that was in her ass a few minutes ago. It plops on the floor by his feet. "Go into the bedroom. Use this."

Daniel just looks down at the dildo. He shakes his head. "I don't think I could…"

Even though Sora is making use of his body, he feels guilty doing anything sexual with hers. It makes him feel like a creep. He is curious about what it would be like, but he doesn't think he can go through with it.

"Just do it," Sora says. "You have to. If you don't understand what gets a woman off by the time we switch our bodies back then we're going to have a problem."

Daniel just picks up the dildo and looks at it. He has no interest in putting that thing inside of him whatsoever. Especially after seeing that it came out of Sora's ass. He smells it to make sure it's clean.

Sora laughs at him as he stands awkwardly with the dildo in his hand. "Just give it a try. You'll figure it out."

*

Daniel locks the door to the bedroom, worried that Sora might walk in on him. He doesn't want her to see him masturbating in her body even though it was her idea.

He finds himself shaking as he takes off his clothes, just as nervous as he was the first time he had sex with Sora. He goes to the bathroom mirror and stares at his naked body. Her skin glistens in the light. He touches his arms. They are so smooth and slick, like they're made of latex. His breasts are so big and blue. He grabs one of them and squeezes. It doesn't feel as pleasurable as he was expecting. Groping Sora's boobs used to turn him on when he was in his own body, but it just feels kind of awkward when he experiences the sensation of being grabbed by his own hand. But his nipples are sensitive and tender. He licks his finger and rubs one until it becomes erect. Still, it doesn't do much to turn him on. It's similar to touching his own nipples when he was a man, only they are quite a bit fatter. The feeling is a little more intense, but not by that much.

He places the dildo down on the sink and reaches for the mound of blue pubic hair between his legs. His long black fingernails poke into the tender flesh on his inner thigh and he pulls his hand away. He lifts his pubic hair back. He can't really see anything at this angle, but he presses his fingers against the

65

opening. When he tries to rub it, his fingers are abrasive against the tender skin and it doesn't feel pleasant at all. He's not really into any of the sensations of touching himself.

He's not sure exactly how to get himself aroused. He feels too awkward to get into it. Even though he can see Sora's sexy body in the mirror, her beautiful eyes staring back at him, he has a hard time imagining the woman in the mirror is his lover rather than himself. He lets out a sigh and removes his hands from his crotch. He bounces his boobs up and down, then lifts them up and makes a goofy face at himself in the mirror, sticking out his tongue and flaring his nostrils. Trying to get turned on by himself while he's in his girlfriend's body just seems stupid to him. He would much rather be watching her while inside his own body.

The sexier he tries to act, the more ridiculous he feels. He plays with his boobs a little more, staring down at them. He squishes them against the mirror and the glass is cold against his nipples. He just feels ridiculous.

But then he presses his lips against the glass of the mirror and sticks out his tongue. When he opens his eyes, he doesn't see himself. He just sees Sora staring back at him. He kisses the mirror as though he's kissing her. He imagines what it would be like if Sora cloned herself and he was in her clone's body while still being able to make love to her while she is in her body.

When he touches his breast, he imagines that it is Sora touching his breast. He puts his hand between his legs and imagines that his fingers are her fingers. While touching his labia, he feels fluids building inside of him. He inserts a finger and coats it with moisture, then he brings his finger to his clitoris and caresses it.

He closes his eyes and focuses on the sensation. It's still a little uncomfortable, but he keeps going. His long fingernails get in the way so he has to move them in a way that they don't scratch his inner thighs. He pulls his breast up to his face and licks his dark blue nipple, trying to wrap his lips around it but he can't quite reach.

As he gets more into it, he feels his muscles tighten inside of him. Then a blob of goo squirts out of him and oozes down his leg. He looks down, wondering what is going on. He hasn't had an orgasm yet. The goo is too thick and creamy to be vaginal fluid or ejaculate. When he opens his eyes to investigate, he sees the green goo dripping out of him and pooling on the floor. It doesn't take long for him to realize that he's leaking poison.

Daniel rushes out of his bedroom, running completely naked into the living room with panic in his eyes.

He jumps in front of Sora's video game, holding up a handful of the green slime. "The poison came out!"

Sora gets annoyed that he got in the way of her video game until she sees the stuff dripping from his fingers. She hits pause and gets to her feet.

"What the hell?" she asks. "That's impossible."

He holds up his hand, his boobs flopping painfully on his chest as he bounces up and down. "It happened! It just came out of me while I was masturbating!"

Sora keeps her distance. "Clean that shit off. Don't get it on anything. You could poison me."

Daniel is too worried to think straight. "What do I do?"

"Just use water. Don't worry about getting it in the sink. It's safe if it gets diluted. But watch where it drips. You want to clean up every drop."

Daniel looks at it and sees it dripping on the ground by his feet. He holds his other hand under to catch it. "Oh shit, oh shit, oh shit..."

Then he rushes back to the bathroom. He spends the next hour cleaning every inch of his apartment that might have the poison fluid on it.

When he's finished, Sora goes to him and says, "I guess you don't know how to control the poison yet. You're like the teenage version of me. That used to happen all the time when I started masturbating."

"I thought adults had total control of their poison."

"I didn't think about how you might not be able to control your glands. It's second nature to me. I never leak my venom unless I intend to."

"What am I going to do?" he asks. "Should we switch bodies back?"

Sora shakes her head. "No, you just have to learn how to control your poison. I'll show you how."

"But that could take forever. I can't be leaking poison everywhere."

"It's fine as long as you don't masturbate or have sex with anyone. Besides, the problem with teenagers not being able to control their poison is that the muscles used to squeeze it out are not developed yet. When we're prepubescent children, we don't have the muscle strength to release the poison at all. As teenagers, we have the muscles but don't have complete control over them so the poison comes out sometimes. But the muscles in my body are fully developed and strong enough. You just don't understand how to operate them."

Daniel doesn't know what to think. He's visibly shaken by the experience, even though he's not in any danger himself while in Sora's body.

"It will be easy once you get the hang of it," Sora says. "I promise you."

*

Daniel spends the rest of the day learning how to control his vaginal muscles. Sora explains that it's not the glands themselves that he has to control. It's the muscles around them. She puts on a lubed up rubber glove and inserts a finger into his vagina to show him where the poison glands are. Daniel cringes as he feels her finger lightly gripping a lump of flesh inside of him. It feels awkward and invasive having her finger inside of him. It's like he's being probed in his intimate places by a doctor. Only the doctor is in his own body. It creeps him out realizing how his fingers feel inside of Sora's vagina from her point of view. He hopes it was never this unpleasant whenever he's fingered her in the past.

"Now use your own finger," she says. She grabs his hand and pushes his index finger inside. The long fingernail cuts at the sensitive flesh in him, but he tolerates it. "Do you feel the gland?"

Daniel feels around the lump. "Yeah, I think."

"Now try to flex the muscles around it. Don't use your fingers. You can actually squeeze the poison out by putting pressure on the gland with your fingers but you don't want to do that. Just use your finger to find the muscle you need to flex."

Daniel squeezes a group of muscles he didn't even know he had. He feels the thick goo squirting onto his finger in a thick stream.

"It's working," he says.

Sora steps back. "Okay stop."

Daniel relaxes his vaginal muscles.

"There's a limited amount of venom so you have to save it. It takes three weeks to produce a new batch and I want you to save what you have left."

"Why don't I just squeeze it all out so it will be safe?"

Sora shakes her head. "No, I want you to learn how to control it. I want you to understand everything there is about being a scorpion."

Daniel nods.

"Now try it without your finger."

Daniel tries again. "I think I've got it."

"To hold it in you mostly just have to avoid putting pressure on the glands. You don't have to use the muscles to hold it in or anything. You just need to learn how to keep your vagina relaxed. When you masturbated, you must have been too tense."

"How will I know if I'm relaxed enough or not?"

"You just have to masturbate more frequently and practice. You'll get the hang of it."

"Did you have to go through this when you were younger?"

Sora nods. "I was taught this at the scorpion ranch. They force teenagers how to control their poison so that they will be safe to be around."

"Shouldn't they know how to control their poison before that? If teenagers were taught how to control their venom then maybe they wouldn't accidentally poison anyone."

Sora laughs. "You're telling me this? Of course they should do that. But adults are so scared of scorpions that they don't want deal with that. They don't even like to accept the fact that teenagers have sex or masturbate at all."

"It's bullshit," Daniel says. "Think of how many lives could have been saved."

Sora smiles at his words. She realizes that he's starting to understand the crap scorpions have to deal with. The body swapping procedure is working. She wraps her arm around him and hugs him tight. Daniel just stands there, holding his hand away from her. He has poison all over his fingers and doesn't want to get any on her while she's groping him within his body.

After he takes a shower and washes the venom off his hands and out of his crotch, he sits down on the couch next to Sora.

"What was it like?" Daniel asks her.

She looks at him with a confused face. "What?"

"The scorpion ranch. I never asked you about it."

Sora becomes uncomfortable with the question and tries to brush it off. Her voice becomes soft. "I try not to think about the scorpion ranch. It was probably the worst part of my life."

"It was that bad?"

Sora shrugs. "It was a fucked up place. The girls there were fucked up. The people running it were fucked up. My parents were fucked up for abandoning me there. I hated every second of it."

"Was it worse than a normal prison?"

Sora just laughs. "Oh yeah. Much worse. The main purpose of the scorpion ranch is to hide venomous women away from the rest of society, to protect boys from our dangerous, deadly, ungodly cunts. They would teach us that we are a poison to civilization, that our genes are poison, that our existence is poison. Those places aren't regulated, so the people running it can do whatever they want without repercussions. Nobody cares what goes on there as long as the public doesn't have to deal with us. In fact, I bet most people would think we deserve everything that happens to us in those places. Most people wish we were killed at birth."

Daniel finds it hard to believe. He thinks she has to be exaggerating. "That's not true. Just because people are scared of your poison doesn't mean they want you all dead."

Sora shakes her head. "Maybe not everyone, but there are plenty of people who feel that way. There wasn't a day that would go by where we weren't told about how hated we are by the rest of society." She pauses and takes a deep breath. "Anyway, I don't want to talk about it. I try to block out that period of my life."

"But you said you wanted me to understand what it's like to be you," Daniel says, showing genuine concern for what she went through. He didn't realize she had such a messed up childhood. "Isn't your time at the scorpion ranch part of who you are?"

71

Sora frowns at him. She doesn't seem to like him digging into her past, despite being the one who insisted on him learning what it means to be a scorpion. She reluctantly tells him more about her experience.

"Fine, but you're going to have to break out some hard liquor for this," she says. "And if I'm a bitch to you for the next few days you'll know exactly why."

It's odd hearing her saying she'll be a bitch for a few days while inside of a man's body, but Daniel doesn't comment on it. He gets a bottle of whiskey from the cabinet above the refrigerator and returns with a couple of glasses.

"So the scorpion ranch I went to didn't look like a prison. It was originally a mental institution. There were eight women per room and we were locked in there for most of the time. We were only let out for three reasons: meals, milking, and education."

"Milking?" Daniel asks, his stomach twisting.

Sora nodded, her expression unreadable. "Yeah, they would milk us of our poison. They would insert tubes into our mouths and vaginas every few days and suck all the poison out of us."

Daniel felt like he might throw up. "Jesus."

She shrugged, "Part of this was for the safety of the staff. In the early days of these facilities, the prisoners would frequently use their poison to attack the guards. They would spit it at them or get it all over their hands to rub it on doorknobs and wipe it across their mouths. After one guard was killed, they came up with the system of milking.

"But it wasn't just about safety," Sora said, her voice intensifying. "Our venom is worth a fortune—medicine, skincare, research. They milked us like cows, drained us dry, and sold it all. We didn't see a single cent. They pocketed the profits and spent as little as possible on us. We barely had food or clothes. No heat, no air conditioning. Showers? Thirty seconds and they timed us. They didn't care if we were clean. They just didn't want to have to pay for utilities."

"Don't they get money from the government?"

"Yeah, but they pocket most of it. Whatever is left goes toward paying the staff. And even then, the guards barely make anything. That's why only the biggest assholes with no experience were in charge of us. They were miserable and took out their frustration on us. Beat us regularly. Almost all of them were men and every single one of them hated scorpions with a passion. Worst human beings I've ever met."

Daniel goes quiet for a moment. He had no idea the experience was that bad. He wants to say something to her, comfort her, tell her about how bad he feels for her for having to deal with that. But he doesn't say anything. He can't find the words.

Before he can speak up, Sora continues, "But the milking wasn't the worst part. It was horrible and dehumanizing, but I got used to it after a while. The education was far worse.

"Every day we were taken into a classroom and forced to endure what I can only describe as an exercise in brainwashing. Some evangelical nutjob would come in and preach to us about how we are freaks of nature who never should have been born. She'd say we were put on earth by the devil to tempt men into sinful pleasure and then kill them so that they would go to hell. All so the devil would have more souls for his army in the war against God. It was some crazy shit."

Sora took a long breath, gripping her whiskey glass. "I hated that woman. She told us that we didn't just have poison in our bodies, we had poison in our souls. She tried really hard to convince us that we were evil. That we should be sterilized to prevent more of us from being born. Having kids, she said, would be the greatest sin we could ever commit."

"And here's the kicker," Sora said with a bitter laugh. "They couldn't legally sterilize us, so they tried to convince us to do it ourselves. That it would be the righteous thing to do."

Daniel stared at her, wide-eyed, but didn't say anything.

"Some of the weaker-willed girls actually fell for her

bullshit. Signed contracts with God, promising to get sterilized at eighteen and have their poison glands surgically removed. That woman had helpers, too—a team of older scorpions who'd been brainwashed long before I arrived at the ranch. They trained the younger girls and taught us how to control our poison glands. But they also bullied us into falling in line. We called them *the tailless* for denying their venomous nature. They were like the Gestapo of the scorpion ranch, the moral police who monitored our every move. All they got out of doing this was slightly better treatment from the prison staff. Nicer rooms with more comfortable beds, better food, and even a movie night once a week. Because of them, the ranch didn't have to hire quite as many prison guards. They were seen as free labor that helped them harvest poison and keep the unruly girls in line. It was a win-win for those in charge.

"The ranch wanted to turn all of us into those brainwashed bitches, but the majority of us didn't fall for it. We had no desire to join the ranks of the tailless. A lot of the prisoners were proud to be scorpions. As I told you before, some scorpions loved being venomous and poisoned their lovers on purpose, just because they could. I was a part of that group, even though I hated all of them. But the tailless left me alone as long as I was with them. They deemed us lost causes and even though we were treated worse than anyone else at the ranch, at least we didn't have to deal with the intense indoctrination that some of the other girls had to go through."

Daniel sits there for a moment as Sora drinks from a full glass of whiskey, staring vacantly at the fireplace.

He doesn't know what else to say but, "I'm sorry you went through all that."

Sora shrugs and takes another sip. She seems pissed off.

She breaks the awkwardness by saying, "Your body can't hold its liquor for shit." She puts her glass down and pushes it way. "I hardly drank half a glass and I'm already shitfaced."

"I'm sorry," Daniel says. He doesn't if he's apologizing for his low alcohol tolerance or her terrible experiences in her youth, but he feels the need to say it again.

"Fuck it," she says. "Whatever doesn't kill you makes you stronger, right? I definitely went into the scorpion ranch a different person than the one that came out. But I'd rather die than ever go back. The ones for adult women are supposed to be even worse. That's why I always think guys are stupid whenever they don't want to be with me just because I'm venomous. Do you really think I'd ever want to go back? If I ever killed a guy in self defense I would have to be able to prove without a doubt that he attacked me. Otherwise it would be considered murder. And when an adult scorpion kills a man she is locked away to be milked for the rest of her life."

Daniel just sips from his whiskey glass, realizing that he was an idiot for never understanding what Sora has had to go through as a scorpion. He wishes he could take back every negative thought he ever had about women like her. He wishes everyone could understand what they go through in the same way that he is beginning to understand. He always thought of scorpions as being tough and fearless. As women who could easily kill a guy if they wanted to, he saw them as having all the power. But they are really more vulnerable than other women. They have far more to worry about in a society that wants them all dead.

CHAPTER
SIX

Being temporarily laid off until he gets his body back, Daniel decides he should get another job in the meantime. Even if it's just for a few weeks, he needs some kind of extra income. Sora told him to just quit his job and find something better, but he doesn't believe he'll be able to get anything worthwhile in such a short amount of time. He sends out his résumé just in case but he doesn't expect to hear back any time soon.

Instead, he tries to get easier minimum-wage work. He applies at the electronics store and the local bank, but the people he hands his application to give him such an evil look that he's sure they throw his application away the second he leaves their sight. When he goes for even worse jobs at the gas station and a few fast-food restaurants, he gets an even worse reaction. One lady is actually offended that he would even apply at her place of work.

She says, "Do you really think I would hire someone like you? I don't want no scorpion handling our food with those disgusting poisonous hands."

"I don't have poisonous hands," Daniel tries to argue.

But the woman just shakes her head. "Our customers would boycott us if they saw you in our kitchen. We don't even want you eating here. Get the fuck out of my sight."

It's the same no matter where Daniel goes to look for work. Nobody wants to hire a scorpion, no matter how desperate they are. He tries working for apps like Uber, DoorDash, or Taskrabbit but after a few orders he gets such bad reviews that he doesn't get any other jobs after that. Nobody wants a scorpion handling their food or driving them anywhere or coming anywhere near their home. Daniel feels like he's fucked. There's no work that he can possibly get while he's in Sora's body. He has no idea how she's survived this long without turning to a life of crime.

"You can do sex work," Sora tells him after he expresses his concern over finding a job.

Daniel freaks out on her. "What? I couldn't do that!"

"It's not that big of a deal. There's this site that specializes in nude scorpion women. You just have to do some photos. Nothing with another person. You'd get like five hundred bucks for a couple hours of work. Do one a week and you'll be fine."

He doesn't know how to respond to that. Posing naked in front of some strange photographer sounds way too awkward. Being in Sora's body rather than his own is a little better. It's not like his friends and family would ever find out that he's done nude photography, but it's still not something that he's at all comfortable with.

"If you really want to know what it's like to be me then you'll give it a shot. It's the only way I was able to make a living for years. The pay is decent and it's not that hard. I'm sure you'd do fine."

"It's really not something I can do. I'm sorry. There's got to be another way to make money in your body."

Sora stares at him with his own eyes, shaking her head. "I want you to just try it once. If you don't like it you never have to do it again."

Daniel shakes his head. There's no way he can do something like that.

"I was just as scared about doing it as you are now," she says. "But I didn't have any other option. Minimum wage jobs never hire venomous women. When you look like me, it's bad for business to put you in front of customers. It's either photosets, camgirl work or stripping, unless you lie on your résumé to get remote working jobs like I did, but that takes months to figure out. In your situation, photosets are the way to go. I already know the people and they love working with me. They've been bugging me for a new set for months. It's your best bet for making money right now."

Daniel tries to find an argument that will shut her down, but he can't think of one. He wishes he would've saved up more money so that he could have survived a month without an income. He wishes he had an emergency fund. But he's never been good with money, not like Sora. She must have learned early on just how important it is for a scorpion to have a lot of savings. But he wasn't prepared. He really doesn't have a choice but to do what Sora did when she was young and desperate. He's going to have to pose naked for perverted men with a scorpion fetish.

"The photographer's name is Jason Chance," Sora tells him. "Don't tell him that you're a man in my body or else he won't want to work with you. He kind of has a crush on me, though he'd never do anything because he's scared of venomous women. Just act like you're old friends and it should be fine. He'll tell you what poses he wants so you just have to follow his instructions until he's satisfied and then you'll get paid."

She drops him off at the photographer's studio and waves him goodbye.

"I think it's kind of hot that you're doing this," she says to him, as he stands on the sidewalk outside her car. "I don't think

I've ever dated a guy who would do something like this just to be with me."

Daniel doesn't respond. He's not doing it for her. He's doing it so that he doesn't get kicked out of his apartment. But there is something about hearing her encouragement that makes it a little easier for him. He likes that he's doing something that earns more of her respect.

"I'll have to check out the set when it goes online," she says, just before she drives off and leaves him standing there by himself.

Daniel walks up the front steps and rings the doorbell. After a couple of minutes, a skinny methhead-looking guy with a blond goatee answers the door. The man's eyes crawl up and down Daniel's body, lingering too long, like he's already imagining him naked. Daniel shifts uncomfortably in his baggy jeans and a hoodie, the fabric doing little to shield him from the man's gaze or from the knowledge of Sora's sexiest black lace underwear clinging to his skin underneath.

The man gives him a big smile that makes him feel violated just by the way he's looking at him.

He says, "Sora! It's been so long! I was worried that we'd never get to work together again."

He goes to Daniel and gives him a big, long, awkward hug.

"I missed you so much," Jason says, grabbing Daniel's ass as he hugs him.

"Umm… yeah, me too." Daniel squirms out of his grasp and steps back. He had no idea that Sora's photographer was so touchy-feely.

"Come in," the photographer says. "I've got everything set up."

Daniel nods and enters the man's home when he opens the door for him.

As Daniel passes him, Jason asks, "What's with that outfit? We can't do a set with that."

Daniel doesn't know what to say. He just walks inside and doesn't look back.

"Don't worry about it," Jason says. "I've got a bunch of stuff you can wear. Are you cool with doing cat girl cosplay? I've always thought you'd look great as a cat girl."

Daniel doesn't want to dress up like a cat girl. He doesn't want to do any of this, actually. But something about acting like a cat doesn't sit right with him.

He responds by asking, "How about if I was a dog girl instead? I'd rather be a dog girl to be honest. I'm more of a dog person than a cat person."

The photographer gets visibly upset. Almost as though he's irritated that Daniel would shoot down his idea, offended that he wanted to be a dog girl instead of his suggestion. He says in annoyed tone, "Yeah, I guess we can do a dog girl set… But let's try doing a cat girl set first. We can do a dog girl set after that."

Daniel regrets opening his mouth. It's like the photographer thinks he's making a compromise by suggesting they do both sets when Daniel doesn't really want to do either. He realizes he has to watch what he says. Being disagreeable only made the photo shoot take longer.

"I'm fine with just a cat girl set, I guess," Daniel says.

Jason's face lights up with excitement. "Oh great! I can't wait to see it!"

He leads Daniel into a walk-in closet full of outfits. From bikinis to costumes to latex body suits, Jason has quite a collection in all different sizes. Daniel thinks there's something a little off about this guy. He likes his job a little too much. He doubts that other photographers would invest their own money into outfits for their models. And when photographing women of all different sizes, it's probably rare that many of the outfits fit them right. But Daniel doesn't even know if this guy is just a photographer or also the owner of the website the photos go on. He seems more like the latter. If Daniel had to bet he'd say this guy doesn't even know much about photography and just pays women to pose naked for him to indulge his own personal sexual fantasies. Daniel can't believe Sora would recommend this guy. He seems like such a weirdo.

"Put this on," Jason says, handing him a cat outfit. It's a calico-patterned leotard with matching ears and tail. "We'll do your makeup next."

Daniel stands there, holding the outfit. Jason just stares at him, as though waiting for him to change.

"Can I get some privacy?" Daniel asks.

Jason laughs. "Privacy? Are you serious? When have you ever been shy about exposing your body to me?"

Daniel doesn't know how to respond to that. He realizes that Sora didn't prepare him well enough for this encounter. He has no idea how she would have behaved in this situation.

His voice trembles when he responds, "Well, I'd prefer to have some privacy this time."

Instead of agreeing like a normal person, Jason changes the subject, "Is something wrong with you, Sora? You're acting really weird. You're not yourself today."

Daniel shakes his head. "I'm sorry. I just don't want to change in front of you."

Jason gets visibly annoyed. "Fine, whatever." He lets out a sigh and exits the closet, closing the door behind him. "Meet me in the bathroom when you're ready."

Jason left the door open a crack, probably on purpose. Daniel has to shut it all the way himself, though the door doesn't lock so he really doesn't feel like he has complete privacy. He really doesn't feel safe getting naked in this closet with the creepy photographer in the other room, but he does it anyway. He tries to change as quickly as he can.

His hands shake as he takes off his shoes and socks, pulls down his pants and underwear, and removes his shirt and hoodie. Then he pulls on the leotard, stepping into it from the top. He's not sure if this is the correct way to put on a leotard, but he can't think of any other way to do it. When he pulls the straps over his shoulders, he feels the g-string thong go up the crack of his ass. He thinks the leotard is a little too small for Sora's body, because it's so tight around the crotch. It gives him a camel toe in the front and painful wedgie in the back. His boobs are so squished in the fabric that his cleavage rolls over the edge of the collar like two beer bellies hanging over a leather belt. When he moves, he feels like he's going to rip the fabric open.

There's a mirror on the inside of the door, but it's foggy and a little distorted. He stares at himself in the leotard and thinks it looks ridiculous on him. He can't imagine Sora ever wearing something like this voluntarily. The calico patterns clash with her aposematic skin. If he picked out his own outfit he would have gone with something that complimented Sora's skin tones. A black cat would have been much sexier than a calico cat.

But even though the outfit is tight and uncomfortable, he doesn't look that bad in it. His boobs look a little too squished together in kind of a gross way but he does think he looks kind of hot. If he was watching porn with a woman wearing this outfit he wouldn't think it was too tight or that her boobs were too squished. He would think it was normal porn attire. It would be weirder if it was too baggy than too tight.

He puts the cat ears on his head and buckles a cat collar around his neck. But when he holds up the cat tail, he can't figure out how to put it on. It takes a few minutes before he realizes what it is. It's a butt plug tail. In order to make it stay on, he has to stick the plug end up his ass.

"Are you fucking serious?" he mumbles to himself, holding

up the plushy calico tail.

He's never shoved anything up his ass before in his life. He has no idea how he's going to get through the set with this. He doesn't have any lube. He knows it's going to be painful and awkward. But the idea of going to Jason and asking to wear something else seems like it would be too much trouble. He takes a deep breath, moves the g-string away from his asshole, and forces it through the constricted ring of his anal sphincter.

Daniel can't walk straight by the time he exits the closet. He wants to cover himself with a robe until they're ready to shoot, but he doesn't see anything to cover himself with. He crosses the master bedroom and sees Jason in there taking a piss with the door open.

"Are you ready?" he asks from the toilet.

"Yeah," Daniel answers, lowering his eyes and hiding on the other side of the door.

After Jason flushes and turns around, a smile stretches across his face.

"Hell yeah, Sora," he says, nodding his head in approval. "You look great in that. I knew you would be a sexy little kitten in that getup."

Daniel ignores his comment. He won't make eye contact with him.

"Let's do your makeup," Jason says, waving him over.

Daniel follows the photographer into the bathroom and lets him draw some cat whiskers on his cheeks and a black upside-down triangle on his nose using an eyeliner pencil.

While he applies the cat features, Jason smells Daniel's hair. He takes a long sniff and then exhales. "You smell different today. Did you change your shampoo?"

Daniel becomes awkward with the question. He has been

using his normal shampoo instead of the stuff Sora uses. She told him explicitly to use her brand so that he didn't mess up her hair, but it's a force of habit to reach for the cheap stuff. He finds it disconcerting that Jason would recognize what kind of shampoo Sora usually uses just by the smell. What kind of creep does that?

"Yeah, I guess so," Daniel says.

Jason picks up a pair of contacts and tells Daniel to put them in his eyes. Daniel opens the case to see yellow cat-like eyes staring back at him. As he tries to figure out how to insert the contacts, Jason begins doing his hair for the shoot.

"By the way, who was that guy who dropped you off?" Jason asks him while brushing his hair, a hint of jealousy in his voice. "Is he a new boyfriend?"

Daniel shakes his head. "No, he's my fiancé."

Jason's jaw drops open. "What the fuck? Are you serious?"

Daniel is confused by his reaction. "Yeah. Do you have a problem with that?"

Jason pulls Daniel's hair tight, shaping it into pigtails. He laughs in a condescending tone. "No, I don't have a problem. It's just I never expected you to actually get engaged. You're not exactly the marrying type."

Daniel wants to knock the guy on his ass. "What does that mean?"

"Well, you're a scorpion for one. For two, you've done way too much porn for a normal guy to have any interest in you. Who is he? Some rich simp who can't get any other girl but a scorpion slut?"

Daniel really wants to stand up and punch him in the face now. He never would have dared say anything like that if Daniel was standing there in his own body. Daniel wants to get in his face about it, tell him off and then storm out of there. But he really needs the money. He decides to let it go for now.

"He's not a simp," Daniel says.

He doesn't say anything else about it.

"Well, I hope he knows what he's getting into. You're too much woman for most guys. I doubt he knows how to handle you."

Daniel just lets it go, ignoring everything the asshole has to say about his relationship with Sora. It's none of his business, anyway. The guy obviously has some kind of crush on his fiancé. Not a serious one. He probably just wants to fuck her but hasn't had the guts to try due to his obvious scorpion phobia. Daniel just wants to get the set over with as soon as possible and tell Sora about what a complete prick he is. He plans to never do a set with him ever again.

Once Daniel has his kitty contacts in and his hair done up like a Japanese Lolita, they start the shoot. He quickly realizes he has no idea how to pose for sexy photos. Unlike Sora, who has years of modeling experience, Daniel feels completely out of his depth. Just standing there naked doesn't cut it. You have to know how to move, how to use your body to arouse interest. It's not just about your tits, it's about seducing the camera with your eyes, your expressions, and the subtle shifts in your posture. Every angle matters, every curve needs to be shown off in the right way. Sora tried to explain all of this to Daniel, but he just didn't grasp how to make it all come together.

Instead of trying to pose in the way Sora told him to, he just does whatever Jason tells him to do. He gets down on all fours with his butt in the air, wagging his butt plug tail. He lets his tongue dangle out of his mouth over a bowl of creamy milk. He lies on his back on the bed with his paws out, as though begging to have his belly rubbed.

From Daniel's perspective, he feels like he's doing a terrible job. He barely puts any effort into his poses. He just comes across as a shy, awkward girl who has no idea what she's doing.

But for some reason Jason eats it all up.

"Holy shit! This is so hot!" Jason has a big smile on his face while he holds the camera, snapping pictures as quickly as he can. "I think this is your best set yet!"

Daniel has no idea what he's talking about, but he continues to pose. The feeling of being in front of the camera is so nerve-wracking that his brain becomes flooded with adrenalin. It makes him feel more in the moment and in touch with his body. It makes him less embarrassed than he was before they started.

When he begins removing his leotard, he barely feels awkward at all. He pulls down just the straps at first, then he frees one of his breasts and presses his tongue to his nipple. He removes his leotard and lets it drop to the floor. Then he stretches out on the bed, hiding his crotch with his hands. Jason moans and cheers with every pose Daniel makes, practically drooling at the sight of him.

Jason won't stop praising him. "I don't know why, but your poses are so much hotter than normal. You look so much more feminine and submissive for some reason. I really like it. Your fans are going to eat this up."

As Jason continues taking photos and ordering Daniel into the positions he wants to see, Daniel notices the bulge growing in the photographer's pants. He tries to ignore it, his eyes focused solely on the camera. But every time Jason grabs at his package, adjusting it to get it in a more comfortable position, Daniel finds his eyes roaming and he can't focus. It doesn't get in the way of Jason praising him repeatedly for being such a sexy little kitten.

"Show me your ass, bend over the bed for me," Jason says, licking his lips.

Daniel does as he asks, but the plug in his ass his really starting to bug him. When he sat on the bed it moved into an uncomfortable position and he has the urge to shit it out right there on the floor.

His face contorts in pain and he asks Jason, "Can I take the butt plug out? It really hurts."

But Jason gets annoyed at him again. "No! Leave it in! Are you crazy?"

Daniel tries adjusting it, moving it in a more comfortable position but he can't seem to find one. "But hurts so much..."

"I want it to hurt," Jason says. "Trust me, it's more sexy that way."

Daniel groans but he doesn't pull it out. For some reason, the more the butt plug makes him squirm the more turned on the photographer becomes. He keeps going despite the pain, trying to do the best he can. He pretends to masturbate while arching his back, grabbing his tits with one hand and cupping his crotch with other, making an expression like he's having an orgasm. Even though it seems so forced and fake to Daniel, the photographer can't get enough. It's like the more awkward Daniel feels, the more he gets praised. He's never felt more exposed and vulnerable in his entire life.

When the set is finished, Daniel rips the butt plug out by the tail, a loud popping sound echoes in the room as it breaks through his sphincter and drops to the floor, covered in some kind of smelly brown mucus.

"Fucking hell..." he says, wiping his ass with a towel.

He rushes to the closet and grabs the clothes he arrived in, not bothering to close the door this time. He just wants to get dressed as soon as possible.

"Damn, Sora," Jason says, following her into the bedroom to watch her getting dressed. "You were amazing. What happened since the last set? Did you get some other modeling experience? You were on a whole new level. I fucking loved it."

Daniel just focuses on getting dressed. When he finishes,

he says, "I don't know. I just did what you asked me to do this time."

"Well, you did it perfectly. The best thing a model can do is give her photographer what he wants." He holds up his fist like he wants to fist bump her. "You leveled up girl. Congratulations!"

Daniel doesn't know why, but he fist bumps him back.

"We need to celebrate. Let's smoke a bowl."

"No, thank you," Daniel says. "I should get going."

"So soon? Don't you want to see the photos first?"

Daniel doesn't know what to say. He just wants to get out of there as soon as possible. "Can you just email them to me? I have to meet my fiancé."

His words piss Jason off. "Fuck him. Hang out for a bit." But when he notices the look in Daniel's eyes, he realizes nothing will convince him otherwise. "Okay, fine. Go to back to your simp boyfriend. I'll email the photos to you when I'm done with them."

On the way out the door, Jason says, "Next time I want to do a bondage set. I think you'd be really hot in a submissive theme. Are you interested? I'm available next week."

"I don't know…" Daniel says, trying to get out of the house.

"The correct answer is yes," Jason says, smiling. He rubs his blond goatee and laughs out loud.

Daniel just forces himself past him and rushes down his driveway to the street.

"I'll see you next week!" Jason yells from his porch. "Same bat time, same bat channel!"

Daniel rushes away from him as fast as he can. He has no intention of ever doing a set with that douchebag again. He walks down the street until he finds a coffee shop. Then he calls Sora and asks her to pick him up.

CHAPTER
SEVEN

After Sora picks Daniel up and takes him home, he tells her all about what happened during the photo shoot. She doesn't seem at all surprised by anything he says.

"Yeah, that sounds like Jason alright."

Daniel is shocked she'd take his story so casually. "You knew that about him and you still worked with him? You still sent me to work with him? He was such a creep."

"Yeah, but all the good photographers don't want to work with scorpions so you're stuck with scumbags like him. But trust me he's way better than the others I've had to deal with. At least he doesn't feel you up between shots."

Daniel can't believe what she's saying. He can't imagine working with a photographer worse than Jason.

"He's really harmless once you get used to him," she says. "I'm sure your next set will go much more smoothly."

"I'm not doing another set."

"Then how are you going to make money?"

"I don't know. I'll think of something."

"Trust me. It's easy work. Dealing with creeps like Jason is far better than working a 9 to 5 surrounded by racists who wish you were dead. If you can even get a job like that this month you'll just be miserable at it. Go ahead and try if you want. You'll learn what I learned when I was younger. People hate having scorpions around."

Daniel shakes his head. He tells her more about his experience. He mentions how Jason got a hard on while taking his pictures. He told her about how much he loved his shots even though he personally thought he did such a horrible job.

Sora just laughs after he tells her this. "See. I told you you'd do fine. I've never been able to do the innocent, vulnerable, submissive woman thing. But I knew you'd be good at it. A lot of the men who work in the porn industry are into that. A lot of porn customers like it, too. But personally I can't stand it and can't do it to save my life. But you probably can. In fact, I bet you'd make a lot of money if you stuck to it."

Daniel shakes his head. "No thanks."

"Who knows? You might grow to love it. A lot of my friends in the porn industry love doing this kind of work. It's kind of demeaning, but it can be empowering, too. There's something appealing about being able to be sexy for a living."

Daniel turns away from her, surprised by her words. Because she's telling him this while in a man's body, he can't help but interpret her words as sexist. Even though she's the one who is actually the woman and he's just a man in a woman's body.

When Jason sends Daniel's payment and a zip file of the photoset, it arrives in Sora's email box. She checks it out the images first and then brings her laptop into Daniel's office.

She says, "Holy shit, Daniel. These pictures are fucking hot."

He takes the laptop and looks at the photos. It's surreal seeing Sora's body posing in the positions he was in. He remembers taking every one of them, but seeing them from Jason's perspective is just strange. He doesn't know why Sora likes them. They don't turn him on in the slightest. In fact, he's embarrassed by them. He can't bring himself to look at them

92

all. Even though he's deeply attracted to Sora's body, he can't see the photos as anything but procedural. They only remind him of the awkward experience he went through in her body.

He pushes the laptop away from him and Sora takes it, staring at them with lust in her eyes.

"You really do look hot in these," she says. "I can see why Jason likes them so much. You're a natural."

Daniel blushes. He doesn't know why, but hearing that come from Sora makes him feel good. He has no plans to ever do a photoset again, but knowing that she appreciates them makes him feel proud of doing a job to her satisfaction.

As she stares at the naked photos of him in her body, she says, "You know, it's weird but I don't see myself when I look at these photos. I only see you. Is that weird?"

Daniel shrugs. "Maybe a little."

"Like I'm totally turned on by seeing you naked. You look like a completely different woman than I was before."

She scrolls through the photos, licking her lips. "I was never really attracted to women before. But for some reason, while I'm in your body, I think I might be becoming a lesbian." She pauses and thinks about it for a minute. "No, I guess I'd be straight now that I'm a man. Either way, I've been seeing women in a different way than I did in my body. Has that been happening to you? Are you finding men attractive now that you're a woman?"

Daniel shakes his head. "Not at all."

"Huh…" She looks up from the screen. "I bet you will eventually. We have different hormones now. It's only natural that we'd be attracted to the opposite genders. Or at least *both* genders."

"There's no way I'd ever be attracted to men."

Sora grabs Daniel by the shoulders and pulls him closer.

"Are you sure?" she asks, staring into his eyes. "You don't find me attractive right now?"

Daniel is repulsed by her words. Of course he's not attracted to her, especially while she's in his body. Although she no longer looks exactly like he did when he was in his own body, he can't help but feel like he's looking into a mirror when she holds him close.

"I don't know…" he says.

"I so want to fuck you right now," she says.

Daniel's eyes widen. "Excuse me?"

She smiles. "I want to fuck you in my body. For some reason, it's really turning me on."

Daniel pulls away from her. "I can't do that."

"Why not? Aren't you curious? We have to try it. At least once. Let's give it a shot."

Daniel shakes his head. "I'm not going to have sex with my own body. That's just too weird."

She leans in and kisses him on the neck. Then she says, "We can put a blindfold on you. You don't have to see who you're making love to." He feels her penis getting erect inside of her shorts as she presses herself tighter against him. "Just let me fuck you. It'll be a new experience to see what it's like to have sex as a woman."

"But being fucked with my own body? That is not a turn on whatsoever."

"Would you rather do it with some other guy?"

"No!"

"Then just give it a shot. Who knows? You might like it."

She pulls out her dick and points it in his face. Daniel closes his eyes and looks away. She just giggles at how uncomfortable it makes him. She grabs his hand and curls his fingers around her shaft.

"Think of it as masturbation," she says, stroking herself with his hand. "You've jerked off this penis plenty of times in your life. What difference does it make now that I'm in your body?"

As Sora says this, Daniel realizes that she has a point. But for some reason, it doesn't feel like his penis to him anymore.

It feels like some other guy's penis. It's a lot larger than it was when he was in his body. It has a different texture. Maybe it's because his hands are now smaller and smoother, but it really seems like somebody else's penis. It's like he's touching the penis of some strange man he doesn't even know.

"Haven't you ever wondered what it would be like to suck your own dick?" she asks.

She pulls his head closer and presses her penis against his lips. Daniel cringes at the texture as it pokes at his gums and he pulls back.

"I don't know if I can control the poison yet," he argues. "I don't think it's safe."

"I trust you," she says, pulling his head back. "You've been practicing, haven't you? You don't release poison when you masturbate anymore. You can do this."

Then she inserts her penis in his mouth and moans out loud. Daniel squirms as he feels his own penis slide against his tongue, inching its way deeper into his mouth.

"You've always liked the fact that I don't have a gag reflex," Sora says. "I want to see what it feels like for myself."

Daniel closes his eyes tight as she drives her penis as far as she can down his throat.

After deep-throating his girlfriend for a few minutes, they go into the bedroom. Daniel takes off his clothes and puts a blindfold on. Sora grabs his boobs and sucks one of his nipples into her mouth and bites down hard. Daniel winces at the sensation.

"Holy shit..." Sora says, as she fondles his breasts. "My boobs are fucking awesome. I had no idea how hot they are."

She takes off her clothes and wraps her arms around him, squeezing his ass with both hands. Then she kisses him deeply, her dick poking him in the belly. The sensation of his own mouth against him makes Daniel feel weird. Sora hasn't been shaving as regularly as he would, so her chin is prickly and abrasive.

"This is so fucking hot," Sora says. "Are you getting turned on?"

Daniel doesn't respond. He really doesn't have anything positive to say about this.

She lays him down on the bed, guiding him into the position she wants him in. Then she crawls on top of him and explores his body with her tongue. Daniel doesn't really understand why she's so attracted to him in her body. He doesn't feel that way about his own body at all. But for some reason, she finds herself incredibly attractive when seeing herself from an outside perspective.

Daniel wonders if Sora's change in libido is because she's a man now. Men get easily turned on and aren't as picky as women. Maybe Sora is just really horny and even seeing her own body is a turn on to her now. It's natural to be sexually repulsed by your own body if you were to have sex with a clone or a twin of yourself, but this isn't the same thing. She has different genes since she's Daniel. She isn't the same person anymore and is attracted to different people than she used to be.

But if that's true, Daniel wonders, why isn't he attracted to his own body? Maybe it's because Sora was never all that attracted to him to begin with. Maybe she was just with him because nobody better was willing to go out with her.

Daniel tries to shake that thought as Sora kisses him all over his body, sucking on his nipples and kissing his neck. She spreads his legs and slides her finger along his inner thighs as she sucks on his stomach. He finds himself getting wet sooner than he expected. Even though he's not turned on by Sora right now, his body is reacting to her motions on top of him.

As she touches his vagina, Daniel lets out an involuntary

moan. She leans in and flicks her tongue over his soft folds. Because it's her body, she knows better than anyone how to give it pleasure. Daniel tightens his fists as she sucks on his labia while caressing his clitoris. He finds himself arching his back, raising himself closer to her mouth. He doesn't even care about the body she's in or the fact that it's a man doing it to him. It feels so much better than when he tried masturbating with himself. He moans out loud and grabs his breasts, twisting his nipples. He doesn't even know why he does it. He just can't help himself.

Sora pulls her mouth away and inserts her penis inside of him. Daniel yelps at the sensation. He wasn't ready for it. The feeling of having his own dick inside of him makes him feel strange and violated, but it doesn't necessarily feel bad. It's gross in so many ways, but he doesn't stop her.

"Oh fuck yeah..." Sora moans, fucking him slowly at first before picking up speed.

Daniel screams as she slams herself into him, fucking him as fast as she can until she explodes inside of him. The sensation of her pulsating member brings him to orgasm as well. She drops on top of him, breathing her hot breath into his neck, kissing his jaw with her scratchy stubble.

"That was so fucking good," she says, giggling. "Holy shit."

Daniel just lies there, breathing heavily, her semen leaking out of him and down his inner thighs. He's in shock from the experience, still in disbelief that he just had sex as a woman, pounded by his own cock, filled with his own cum.

"I could get used to this..." Sora says, rolling over to the other side of the bed to take a nap.

But Daniel isn't sure how he feels. He really liked the oral sex. He would definitely do that again. However, he's not sure about the rest of it. For some reason, it makes him feel kind of gross.

He feels a burning sensation inside of his pussy. Sora had been eating a lot of spicy food lately so her cum burns.

He rushes to the bathroom to urinate and wash himself out, cringing at the pain.

They have sex a lot more over the next few days. Because neither of them have to go to day jobs, they can just stay home and fuck all day. Sora doesn't bother masturbating anymore. Whenever she gets an erection, she just grabs Daniel, bends him over the couch and fucks him doggy style or pulls him into the bedroom and slams his brains out. She hasn't been giving him oral sex as much anymore, just enough to get him ready for her penis. Daniel is a little disappointed that she's not spending as much time on him in bed. She doesn't even make sure he has an orgasm before she pulls out and goes back to playing video games.

He is getting used to having sex with Sora while she's in his body. It's not so awkward anymore. He doesn't even have to wear the blindfold. The more he makes love to her, the less he sees her as himself. His body is molding to her like a baseball glove, changing shape, becoming a part of her. He sees her as a completely different man from himself. And he's beginning to feel like Sora's body is his own. He's becoming comfortable in her skin. He isn't Sora, he's some other scorpion woman he's never met before. It's like they both are two new people in a completely different relationship then they were when they first met. He's not sure he's happy with the change but it's becoming the new normal.

He's sure he can get through this. He's only got ten days left. It won't be long before he's back in his own body again.

CHAPTER
EIGHT

Daniel is supposed to do another shoot with Jason today. He doesn't want to go, but Sora pressures him into it. He hasn't tried looking for another job, feeling like there's no hope in finding other work as a scorpion. He's been trying to save money, trying not to spend much on food or alcohol. Sora tells him he's getting too skinny and thinks he's hotter when he has more meat on his bones. But Daniel says she can just gain the weight back once they switch bodies at the end of the month.

She drops him off at Jason's house and says, "Good luck. I'm excited to see how hot you look in the next photoset."

Daniel just groans at her and she laughs. Then she speeds off, leaving him at the creepy photographer's doorstep.

When Jason lets him inside, he says, "Oh shit, you actually showed up! I thought you were going to ghost me like you normally do."

"I need the money," Daniel says, stepping into his living room. The place is a shithole. It doesn't look like the guy cleaned up at all since the last time he was there.

"Don't we all?" Jason says, locking the front door behind them. "I'm glad you came. This next set I have planned is going to be amazing. Did you check out the photos I sent you from last time?"

Daniel nods. "Yeah, my fiancé really liked them."

He says this on purpose just to remind the creep that he's in a serious relationship. His words clearly irk Jason, but the asshole doesn't say anything in response.

Jason just shakes his head and says, "Well, these are going to be even better. You're going to be a sub in a bondage set. Since you wanted to be a dog girl last time, I figured we go with the dog girl theme but from an S&M angle. You'll be a sexy little pet puppy who's been a bad dog and deserves punishment. I even bought a new outfit for you. You're going to love it. I promise."

Daniel wants to throw up. This set sounds even worse than the last one. He's always been disturbed by guys who are turned on by women in bondage. Watching a video of a woman getting tied up until she's helpless and vulnerable while men have their way with them always made him feel gross and creepy. He really doesn't want to have anything to do with this kind of thing. But he wants to get paid so he doesn't object. He just hopes to get it over with as quickly as possible.

Jason gives him the dog girl outfit and Daniel puts it on in the closet. It can barely be considered an outfit. It's just a black latex hood with dog ears and a muzzle, a harness that crosses between his boobs, a dog collar with a shiny bone-shaped dog tag, and matching thong underwear with a zipper in the crotch.

When Daniel steps out into the living room, Jason just gives him a slow clap, completely impressed by his own choice in fetish attire.

"Perfect!" Jason cries. "Absolutely perfect!"

Daniel feels weird having his boobs just hanging out like they are. He has only two black heart-shaped pasties covering his nipples, but his breasts are otherwise fully exposed.

Jason points to the bedroom. "Let's get started. I'm so enthused right now. I've been waiting all week for this."

Daniel is on all fours on the floor, a big plastic bone in his mouth. He is squatting down and making a growling face at the camera. Jason has him on a leash, holding it in one hand while taking photos from the other. Jason is filming as though he is a character in the photoset, making it seem like the audience is interacting with Daniel the dog girl through him. Jason's hand is the viewer's hand.

He has Daniel pose with a ball in his mouth, then a frisbee. He tells him to sit, roll over, and then play dead. He gives Daniel a doggie treat which Daniel has to pretend to eat and enjoy, expressing appreciation to his master. Jason pets his head and says, "Good girl," even though his voice can't be captured on a photograph.

Jason uses his own hands to remove the pasties from Daniel's nipples, his fingers lingering a little too long as they brush against his breast. He has him unzip his latex panties and show off his bright blue pubic hair poking out of the slot. After a few more pictures, Daniel removes the underwear completely. He's told to leave on the rest of the outfit.

Then Jason tells Daniel to raise one of his legs and pretend that he's peeing on the bedpost. He's supposed to be a girl dog, but Jason thinks it's hotter for him to pee like a male dog. He says nobody will understand if he pees like a female.

Jason points a finger at him and says, "Bad dog! No peeing! Stop!"

Daniel gives him sad puppy dog eyes, expressing shame in the way a dog would when they get yelled at by their owner. He lowers his head in submission.

Jason laughs. He is having the time of his life. "Now you have to be punished."

He has Daniel bend over the bed and spanks his bare ass. Daniel doesn't really think it's that big of a deal, even though it's awkward as fuck. But on the third smack, Jason squeezes his butt cheek.

Daniel gets annoyed. "Hey, cut it out."

Jason giggles. "It's just for the audience. They love this kind of thing." But he doesn't do it again. "Get on the bed. I'm going to tie you up now."

Daniel poses for the camera as he obediently climbs onto the bed and assumes the position. Jason photographs himself tying Daniel's wrists and ankles to the bed posts.

"Don't tie them too tight," Daniel says. "I don't need to actually be bound to the bed."

Jason waves off his words. "I want it to look authentic."

He tightens the bonds until Daniel squeals at the pain. It only makes Jason happier. He wants to make him cringe. He wants him to be completely at the camera's mercy.

Jason continues snapping shots as Daniel writhes on the bed, pretending to struggle against the bonds. But it quickly gets boring. There's not much he can do while his arms and legs are tied up. Jason picks up the plastic bone from the floor and puts it in his mouth, but it doesn't do much for him. He takes the bone out and then starts rubbing Daniel's boobs with it, wetting his nipples with his own dog drool. Then Jason tosses it aside and uses his hand, groping Daniel's boob and squeezing it as hard as he can.

"What the fuck!" Daniel screams. "Don't fucking touch me!"

Jason gets annoyed by his words. "I'm just trying to make a good set."

Daniel fights against the ropes, trying to pull his hands out. "I didn't say you could touch me, asshole."

Jason rolls his eyes. "I'll pay you more. Just let me do my job."

The photographer takes pictures as he fondles Daniel's breasts. The dog girl tries pulling his breasts away, putting all of his strength into getting a hand out of the ropes in order to push the photographer away. But his struggles only make Jason do it more.

"Yeah, this is getting good now," the creep says. "Show me

how much of a bad dog you are."

"Stop it, you piece of shit!"

Jason just laughs. He gets closer to Daniel's face and removes his dog mask. Then he unzips his fly and pulls his dick out.

"Suck it," he says.

Daniel can't believe this is happening to him. It doesn't feel real, like some kind of sick joke is being played on him. He moves his head away, his face flush with anger. "Get that away from me!"

Jason doesn't back off. "Come on. I'll pay you double. It's just for the set."

"I'm serious."

Jason pushes it closer, poking it into the side of his neck.

"You're so fucking hot, Sora. You've always been such a tough chick. I honestly wasn't really that into you before. But now you're different. Acting all shy and sexy. You're just the kind of girl I like working with."

Daniel doesn't know what else to do. He can't get out of his bonds. He has no choice but to tell him everything.

"I'm not Sora!" he cries.

The photographer looks at him.

"I'm her fiancé, Daniel. We switched bodies. I'm only doing this because I need the money."

Jason just laughs. "Bullshit. What kind of joke is that?"

"I'm serious! I'm really a man."

The photographer laughs harder. "No, you're not. All I see is a hot scorpion bitch tied up in my bed."

Daniel doesn't know if the creep thinks he's lying or realizes he's telling the truth but doesn't care.

"Come on, I want to make the best set ever." Jason squeezes Daniel's cheeks, forcing them open so that he can stick his dick inside.

"If you don't get that away from me I'll poison you," Daniel yells, his words muffled with Jason's hands gripping his face. "I'll fucking kill you!"

Jason freaks out on him for saying that. "What the fuck did you just say? You'd actually kill me for this? Fuck you, you scorpion cunt."

Jason gets off of him and leaves the room. For a moment, Daniel thinks he's safe. He scared the guy off. He relaxes for a bit, hoping the guy can settle down and finally release him from his bonds. But when Jason comes back, he's holding a gun in his hand.

"We're doing this, bitch," Jason says.

He crawls onto the bed and presses the barrel of the handgun to the side of Daniel's forehead. Then he says, "If you try to poison me I'll blow your brains out. You'll die before I do. So just stop being a cunt and suck my dick."

Daniel tenses up, his mind in too much of a panic to think straight. He has no idea what to do. He knows that if he could convince the asshole that he'd rather die than go through with it then he'd scare him off, but he's not actually willing to die. He's not threatening enough. He doesn't know how to bluff. If he was the real Sora he would know how to handle this. She could get out of this no problem. But Daniel's weak. He's a far weaker woman than her.

He tries to plead with Jason. "You don't want to do this. I don't know how to control my poison. This isn't my body. I might poison you by accident."

But Jason doesn't listen. He shuts Daniel up by shoving his weird, shriveled, narrow penis into his mouth and fucks his face, taking pictures of every second it, until he cums. He pulls out and shoots his load all over Daniel's face, on his tongue, in his eye, even up his nose. Daniel gags and chokes, but it only makes the asshole laugh.

When he's finished, Jason gets off of him and looks at the photos on his camera, a big smile on his face.

"I think that went really well," he says. "I liked that even better than the last one."

Then he leaves the room.

When Jason comes back, he pretends that nothing happened. He unties Daniel and lets him get to his feet.

Daniel leans forward and blows the cum out of his nose and cleans his face with the bedsheet. Then he rips off his outfit and goes to his clothes, trying to get dressed as fast as he can.

Jason pours himself a beer and raises his glass. "Here's to another amazing set."

He takes a sip and sets the glass down. Then he goes to the other room to load the photos onto his computer.

Daniel looks down at the glass. Anger is filling his eyes. He squeezes poison from the glands in his mouth and fills his cheeks. He picks up Jason's glass, getting ready to spit in it. He wasn't able to poison him while the gun was to his head, but he can still poison him this way.

But before he spits it out, Daniel hesitates. He starts to think of the consequences of going through with it. If Jason actually drank the poison and died, he would be charged with murder. He would be sent to the scorpion ranch like Sora was. Or maybe she would, if she was arrested after they changed bodies back. Daniel just swallows the poison and puts the glass down.

He heads for the front door. When he runs into Jason, he tells him, "You're paying me triple for that."

Jason just laughs at him. "No I'm not. I'll pay you double, like I said. Be happy with that."

"You fucking raped me!"

Jason gets annoyed by her words. "Oh, don't exaggerate. I was just trying to save a photoset that you were fucking up. You're lucky I'm paying you at all."

Daniel shakes his head. "Fucking asshole… I should call the cops."

He goes to the door and fumbles to open the lock, too upset to figure out how it works.

Jason stares at him as he tries to leave, sipping on his beer with a smug look on his face. "Yeah, like the police will give a shit about some scorpion whore."

When Daniel gets the lock to work, he throws open the door, steps out, and slams it behind him.

Daniel tries calling Sora, but she doesn't answer her phone. He goes to the nearby coffee shop where he was picked up last time, but Sora doesn't show. She still isn't answering her phone.

He calls an Uber and goes home. When he walks through the front door, he sees Sora naked in the living room with another woman. It's the young blonde girl who lives across the hall. Sora's fucking her with her legs over her shoulders, pounding her with fury. Both of them are grunting and screaming. The walls are shaking, rattling the paintings and knocking books off of the bookshelves.

Daniel can't believe his eyes. At first, he thinks he had to have walked into the wrong apartment. But it's his living room. It's his couch. It's his body. That girl is barely nineteen. What the fuck is Sora thinking?

"Sora?" he asks in the meekest tone he's ever heard come from his lips.

She looks back at him just as she has an orgasm. It's too late to stop, past the point of no return, so she finishes herself off as she stares at Daniel with surprise in her eyes.

"Daniel? What are you doing here?"

"You never picked me up," he says. "What the hell are you doing?"

The blonde woman freaks out when she sees the pissed off scorpion woman standing before her. She was always such a nice girl to Daniel. He can't believe she'd do that to him. She doesn't know that she was having sex with Sora in his body, but she might be starting to understand now that they are calling each other by the wrong names.

"Daniel, this isn't what it looks like," Sora says.

The girl gets her clothes and rushes out of the apartment, giving Daniel a wide berth as she passes him, not wanting to get too close to the angry scorpion woman.

"How could you do that?" Daniel asks.

Sora slowly puts her clothes back on. "It just happened. I wanted to see what it would be like to have sex with a woman in a man's body."

Daniel points at himself. "But you've already been having sex with me. You already know what it's like to have sex with a woman."

She shakes her head. "Yeah, but you're in *my* body. It's not the same. And I wanted to see what it would be like to have sex with a woman who wasn't venomous, who didn't have my skin tones. I've never been with one before. It was really fun!"

Daniel doesn't take it lightly at all. "But you used my body! How could you do that? Did you even use a condom? What if you gave me an STD?"

Sora gets annoyed by his tone. "She didn't have any STDs. Don't be so overdramatic. I'm only going to be a man for another week or so. I had an opportunity and just wanted to see what it would be like."

Daniel doesn't know what to say. He's so pissed off at her right now. After what had just happened to him, he needed her now more than ever.

Sora sees the look on his face and calms down. "Look, I'm sorry." She pats the couch next to her, beckoning for him to sit down. "Come here."

Daniel goes to her.

She wraps her arms around him when he sits down.

"I don't care about that person. I only want to be with you." She pulls back and looks him in the eyes. "Tell you what. Why don't we have you sleep with somebody else? Then we'll be even."

Daniel shakes his head. "I don't want to have sex with a man."

"Well, what about a woman?" Sora asks. "Haven't you ever been curious about what that would be like? I'm sure you would love it."

Daniel is just annoyed by her words. There was a time where that idea would appeal to him, but right now it just sounds gross.

"I can hook you up with my ex-girlfriend. I'm sure she'd go for it. She's still in love with me and always tries to get me to agree to a booty call. You'll have a lot of fun. I promise."

"I don't know. I don't really feel like it. I only want to be with you."

Sora gets annoyed. "Come on. We won't be even unless you do it. I want you to."

She picks up her cell phone and starts texting someone. Daniel just lets out a sigh. He's so upset by everything that happened today that he just wants to scream.

After the date is set up with Sora's ex-girlfriend, Daniel gives her the silent treatment for over an hour. She tries to comfort him, kissing him on the cheek and holding him close to her. Then he tells her everything that happened to him with Jason that day.

Sora gets even more pissed off than Daniel about it.

"Are you fucking kidding me?" she yells. "That asshole did *what?*"

Daniel tells her again.

"Why didn't you kill his fucking ass?" she yells at him, acting just as mad at Daniel as she is Jason, blaming him for letting it happen to her body.

"He had a gun. There was nothing I could do."

"Do you think having a gun matters? The poison would have paralyzed him instantly. He wouldn't have been able to pull the trigger if he tried."

"I didn't know that."

Sora puts on her shoes and her coat. "That motherfucker's dead."

"What are you doing?"

"Stay here. I'm going to fuck his ass up."

Then she storms out of the apartment.

Sora returns with her knuckles all swollen and bloody, the skin peeling off so much that it hurts just to look at. She doesn't say anything about what happened, but Daniel can tell that she beat the hell out of Jason.

She slams a wad of cash on the coffee table. "This is for you. He said he was sorry and would never do it again."

Daniel looks at the money on the table. It has to be about five thousand dollars, probably all the cash the guy had on him.

"Are you serious?" he asks.

Sora just nods and goes into the bathroom to wash her hands. Daniel can't believe she did that. He never could have done something like that for her if he was in his body. She's so much more manly than he was, so much stronger and confident. He's not sure why, but he kind of feels turned on by her right now. He can't help but jump all over her and take her into the bedroom, totally forgetting about all the horrible things that happened that day.

CHAPTER
NINE

With all the money he has now, Daniel doesn't have to worry about doing another photoset or getting a second job. He has more than enough to last until after he gets his body back and can go back to work. He still would have preferred not to have gone through what he did, but at least he got something out of it. If it wasn't for Sora it wouldn't have worked out so well. But he hasn't yet forgiven her for fucking another woman. He's feeling weird about the whole situation, even weirder than he did before the switch. He's looking forward to getting his body back.

He isn't able to wiggle out of his date with Sora's ex-girlfriend. She must have felt really guilty about what she did. She's only doing this so she will feel better about herself and Daniel's only doing it so that she will feel better about herself. But he'd prefer if Sora made up for it by just showing him more attention and affection. All he wants is for her to prove that she actually loves him. She's never even said that to him before and it's beginning to make him feel rejected. He wants to marry her now, he's sure of it, but he needs to know how she really feels about him. Having him fuck her ex-girlfriend is not the way to do it. In fact, it kind of makes him feel like things are going in the wrong direction. Like she wants to drive them apart.

The woman's name is Tia, another scorpion woman like Sora. Daniel meets her at the same brewery where he met Sora on their first date. She is a strange-looking woman, even for a scorpion. She has a smooth bald head and piercings everywhere on her face, through her eyebrows, septum, lips, nostrils, dimples, and dozens in her ears. She comes across a lot trashier than Sora, but isn't exactly unattractive. She's shorter, rounder, and has bigger boobs than Sora, though they sag really low on her stomach. He can't tell if she's in her early twenties or late forties, but she presents herself like she's still a teenager. Her aposematic skin isn't as pretty as Sora's. She is really splotchy with patches of red, black and yellow, mostly yellow, which is Daniel's least favorite color.

When she meets him, she has a bubbly personality, hugging him like they've known each other for ever.

"You're Daniel, right?" she asks, gripping his shoulders tightly and speaking directly into his face. "Sora told me all about your situation. It's really cool you'd switch bodies with her. I've never known anyone who'd have the guts to body swap with a scorpion. You must really love her to go through this."

Daniel is surprised she knows that he's not really Sora. His fiancé didn't tell him that she would know it was really a man in her body. He feels kind of relieved that he doesn't have to put up an act. It makes it so much easier. But still, he wonders what kind of woman would still be interested in sleeping with him despite knowing that he's not the person that she's actually into.

"Shall we go inside?" Tia asks.

When they enter the brewery, the customers are even more freaked out than the time he met with Sora here before. He guesses that two scorpion women are even more threatening than just one. Perhaps having a human buffer between them and his date made it a little more tolerable.

The bartender asks them for the order from across the bar as though no waiter wants to approach them, so Tia tells them what they want, ordering for the both of them. She just asks for the strongest beers they have and the bartender nods his head.

"So you don't mind that I'm not really Sora?" Daniel asks her.

She shrugs and gives him a smirk. "I thought it was kind of cool that she wanted me to have sex with her body, even if it's just her boyfriend inside of it. Don't get me wrong, I love Sora. But she's kind of too into herself. She never opens up. She's hot as fuck. *You're* hot as fuck. But we never really clicked. Her body with a different personality is something I find intriguing. I love the idea of going on a date with a different version of her, even if it's not the real Sora."

When their beers are ready, they have to stand up and get them for themselves, taking them from an empty part of the bar where no one else will have to breathe their same air.

They sit back down and continue chatting.

Daniel asks, "So how long have you known Sora?"

"Since we were kids," Tia says. "We were at the scorpion ranch together. She told you about that, right?"

Daniel nods. "She mentioned some things about her time there. What was she like back then?"

Tia giggles and rolls her eyes back like she's already drunk after only a sip of beer. "Oh, don't get me started. She was such a tough bitch back then. All the guards were terrified of her, even after she had her poison drained. She didn't need venom glands to fuck someone up. She clawed the eyes out of some tailless bitch who pissed her off and then turned on the guards that tried to break them up. She kicked this guy in the nuts so hard that he never came back to work ever again. Not because he was injured but because he was too fucking scared to ever go near a scorpion like Sora ever again."

Daniel is shocked to hear this. Sora hadn't said anything about this before. But he can totally imagine her being that kind of person, especially after what she did to Jason.

"I don't think I would have gotten through my time there if it wasn't for Sora. She really looked out for her friends. I was so in love with her back then."

Daniel just nods his head. He doesn't really want to hear about her relationship with his fiancé, but Tia tells him every gory detail. She fills them in on their sex life, how they used to live together for a few years after they left the scorpion ranch, how they survived stripping and then doing porn. How they had no one else in the world but each other until Sora decided she didn't want to be a lesbian anymore and wanted to do something more productive with her life.

"Sora was kind of a nerd, always reading books and messing around on her computer. She always looked to the future and it pissed me off because I knew she didn't see me as a part of it."

Even though he doesn't like the idea of their relationship, Daniel finds himself empathizing with her.

"What about you?" Tia asks. "How did you fall in love with Sora?"

Daniel tells her the whole story. For some reason, he's completely honest with her. He even tells her about how he really didn't know if he loved her, how he wasn't sure he wanted to marry her until recently. But Tia doesn't judge him. She just nods her head, completely understanding where he's coming from.

Then she changes the subject out of nowhere. "I've never had sex with a guy before. This is going to be my first time. You're not in a guy's body right now, so maybe it doesn't really count, but it's still new for me. I'm more into girls than guys, but I've always been curious. I could never sleep with a real guy. I can't even sleep with a normal woman. I'm quite a bit more poisonous than other scorpions so I can only have sex with other scorpions."

"More poisonous?"

She smiles at him and then chugs her beer. "Let's go back

to my place and I'll show you."

The reason Tia is more poisonous than other scorpions is because she has no control over her poison. She was never able to figure out how to control her muscles. They tense up too easily, against her will, even when she's not engaged in sexual activity.

When Daniel gives her oral sex, she fills his mouth with her poison, discharging it across his chin and down his throat. And when she kisses him, she squirts venom through his lips. The thick substance feels like she's throwing up in his mouth. Her tongue spreads it across his labia as she licks him, covering his body with so much poison that it could probably kill anyone who came in contact with him. He quickly realizes that scorpions like Tia are the ones that normal people are so afraid of.

After Daniel has an orgasm, Tia crawls on top of him and wraps her arms around his quivering body. She droops her saggy yellow breasts over his bright blue stomach and lies her smooth head against his chest, listening to his heartbeat. They lay in silence for a few minutes. Tia just holds him, imagining that he's the real Sora, trying to pretend for just a few minutes that she's with her again. Then she begins to cry.

Daniel can't say he really liked the experience. It was new and different, but he would much prefer to have been with Sora again, even while she is in his body. But he promised her he would give having sex with Tia a shot. Now they're even and he never has to sleep with another woman ever again.

After sleeping with Tia, Daniel thought it would be over. They could get on with their relationship, Sora's infidelity all forgiven. But the second Daniel went through with having sex with her ex-girlfriend, Sora started acting like they had an open relationship. She continued having sex with the blonde across the hall. She went on dates with girls she met online. She even picked up a guy at a gay bar so she could feel what it was like to try anal sex as a man. He almost feels jealous that she's able to get so many girls to sleep with her. He was never able to do that. How is she able to pick up so many women using the same body that he failed with so many times before? She doesn't even shave or bathe as much as he did. She's even put on weight. Yet she's able to get any woman she wants. He doesn't understand it.

Sora would never tell Daniel what she was doing when she would leave the house for hours or sometimes days on end, but she didn't keep it a secret. She encouraged him to call up Tia and have sex with her again, but she never mentioned why she wanted him to even though it obvious. The more he slept with Tia the more she could sleep with other women. She forced an open relationship on them that he never wanted.

When it's time for them to switch bodies back, Sora says that they can't do it yet. She explains that the doctor isn't available and has rescheduled them for another two or three weeks. This pisses off Daniel to no end. He tells her that he needs his body back. He needs to go back to work. But she says there's nothing she can do.

Daniel emails his boss about the situation, but he doesn't hear back from him. He wonders if his company has already replaced him and doesn't expect him to ever come back. Maybe they think he's a risky employee if he's marrying a scorpion. He could get poisoned at any time, perhaps in a moment when they really needed him. He wonders if they wanted an employee who was more likely to be around for a longer amount of time and bring a spouse to company picnics or holiday parties that wouldn't poison all the other employees.

Although he has no proof, Daniel suspects Sora is lying to him about the doctor. He believes she rescheduled the procedure on purpose because she's having so much fun in his body that she's not ready to give it back. She has been going out a lot more than she used to, going out to pubs and movies and concerts and all the places she was never able to go to as a scorpion. She's realizing what life can be like when she's not hated by everyone around her.

She hasn't been having sex with Daniel at all lately. She has only done it with him once in the past couple of weeks and that's just because he made her feel guilty about it. He can't believe how pathetic it is to beg to be pity-fucked by his own body. He realizes he's spending more time with Tia than his own fiancé. At first, he went to her as a way to get back at Sora for sleeping with so many other women, but after the third night with Tia he doesn't seem like he's punishing Sora. He just feels like he's punishing himself. He's only making it easier for Sora to sleep around without feeling bad about it.

But he's finding Tia more attractive whenever he spends the night with her. Even though her black and yellow boobs look like wasp butts, he still enjoys sleeping with her. Not having to worry about being poisoned when having sex with a scorpion woman is really freeing. Though it really doesn't compare to being with his fiancé.

After about seven weeks in Sora's body, Daniel begins to feel sick. He's throwing up when he wakes up most mornings, not sure why he feels so shitty all the time.

"When did you have your last period?" Tia asks him after

he throws up in her bathroom after he spent the night at her place.

Daniel looks up at her, a confused look on his face. He doesn't know why he hasn't thought about that before. He's been in a woman's body for almost two months. Of course he should be having periods.

"I have no idea," he tells her. "I haven't had a period since I entered Sora's body. I don't even know what it's like."

Tia lets out a long sigh. "I don't know how to break it to you, dude. But I'm pretty sure you're pregnant."

"What!" Daniel cries. "No way... That's impossible..."

Tia can't help but laugh at him. "You have a womb now, bud. It's one hundred percent possible."

She goes to the store and gets a pregnancy test for him. He pees on the strip and it comes up positive.

"Oh fuck..." Daniel says, staring down at the two pink lines.

Tia smiles and pats him on the shoulder, completely amused by his situation. "Congratulations, man. You're going to be a mother!"

Daniel drops his head on the toilet seat, feeling like the biggest idiot in the world.

When he tells Sora about it, she freaks out on him.

"What do you mean you're pregnant?" she yells.

Daniel cowers when she raises her voice. She really is intimidating as a man. "I took a pregnancy test. It's positive."

"What? How?"

"It's yours," Daniel says, then he shakes his head. "I mean mine. It's ours."

"How is it possible? You're on birth control."

"Birth control?" he asks.

Her jaw drops. "Are you telling me you weren't taking my pills?"

"You never told me I was supposed to! I didn't think about it."

"How the fuck could you not think about it? Of course you needed to take them."

"I didn't even think we were going to have sex while we were in each other's bodies."

"Don't blame me for this. You fucked up."

Sora paces around the room, kicking shoes and books across the floor. "I can't believe you got my body pregnant. I'm not ready to have a kid."

"We could have an abortion," Daniel says. "It's illegal here, but we can fly to Oregon. I think you can still get them there."

Sora shakes her head. "I don't believe in abortion."

"I thought you were pro-choice?"

"I *am*, but I'm pro-life when it comes to *my* baby."

"It's no problem," Daniel says, trying to comfort her. "I can get a flight next week. I still have the money from Jason. It'll be no big—"

She cuts him off by grabbing him by the shoulders and slamming him against the wall. "Don't you even think about aborting my baby! You hear me?"

Daniel is so alarmed by her anger that he starts to cry. He's not sure if it's his hormones or what, but he's just so overwhelmed that he can't help himself. Sora lets him go and he slides down the wall and wraps his arms around his knees, tears flowing down his cheeks.

Sora just rolls her eyes at Daniel's behavior. She doesn't apologize or acknowledge what he's going through.

She just says, "You're the one who's going to have the baby."

Daniel looks up at her, not sure what she means by that.

Sora glares down at him. "This is your fault, so you can deal with the childbirth. I don't want to go through that shit."

"Are you fucking kidding me?" Daniel cries. "You want me

to have the baby?"

"I think it's only fair."

"But I want my body back. I'm sick of being a woman. I'm going to lose my job. What am I going to do about money?"

Sora sighs. "Don't worry about it. I make enough for both of us. Just focus on having the baby and I'll take care of you."

Then Sora grabs a bottle of whiskey and leaves the apartment. She's probably going across the hall to fuck the blonde who lives there. Daniel buries his face in his knees. He has no idea what he's going to do.

CHAPTER
TEN

Daniel doesn't adapt well to pregnancy. His moods are erratic and unpredictable. He goes from feeling euphoric to depressed, from feeling angry to crying at the tiniest thing. His breasts are tender and swollen. His stomach is stretching and he's beginning to put on weight.

Sora is just as moody as Daniel is. Sometimes she's extra loving, bringing him pillows to help him get more comfortable or buying him chocolates and flowers to show him how much she loves him. She touches his stomach, excited for the day when she'll be able to actually feel her baby growing inside of him. But other days, she gets annoyed with Daniel for being such a pain in the ass.

She glares at him and shakes her head, saying, "That thing is going to destroy my figure."

She still can't stop blaming him for getting her body pregnant, even though she was the one who blew her load into him every chance she had, without even thinking about the consequences. It was her body. She should have known he wouldn't have the knowledge to take care of it the same way she would. He's not the only one to blame.

Sora still goes out and fucks other people, but not as much as she did before. She doesn't let Daniel drink or smoke pot with her. She doesn't like it when he leaves the house by himself and doesn't want him to hang out with Tia.

Tia has been texting him frequently since she found out he was pregnant. She has become his only friend outside of his relationship. She seems to really care about what he's going through, although she seems more amused by it than anything. She finds it funny that someone who has born a man is actually going through a pregnancy. She wants to know all the gory details about how he's dealing with it. She even helps research things online that will help him cope with his situation. She's even more useful to him than Sora these days.

But Sora is keeping her side of the deal. She's making enough money to pay for both of them and hasn't complained once about being the sole provider. All Daniel has to do is worry about carrying her baby to term and then he has to give birth to it.

Daniel has to see a special doctor to get proper medical care. Most doctors don't want to deal with scorpion mothers. It's very common for scorpions to release poison when they give birth. As they squeeze the muscles to push the baby out, it's almost guaranteed to trigger the same muscles that control the venom. It's dangerous for the doctors and even more dangerous if the baby is a boy who doesn't have an immunity to the poison. The procedure is very complicated and requires a specialist who knows how to ensure the safety of all involved.

The first time he meets his obstetrician, Daniel is surprised that he doesn't have any awkwardness over him being a scorpion whatsoever. The doctor works with venomous women all the time, so he's not scared of them in the slightest. He understands their biology better than anyone and knows how to be safe around them, even when dealing with their poison. Like a rattlesnake handler, once you know how to deal with a venomous creature you no longer have to fear them. Daniel wishes everyone in the country could learn that knowledge from this man.

"Your baby's very healthy," he tells Daniel. "You don't have anything to worry about."

"What's the gender?" Sora asks. It's all she's been wanting to hear since they got there.

"Are you sure you want to know?" He looks at Daniel, wanting his permission before telling them.

The doctor has no idea that Daniel is really a man in a woman's body. Daniel wanted to tell him but Sora wouldn't allow it. Because they did the body swap illegally it would get them into trouble if they told anyone. The doctor would be forced to report them.

Daniel nods his head at the doctor. "What is it? A boy or a girl?"

The doctor smiles. "Well, in my opinion it's good news. It's a girl. That will make the birth so much safer and easier for us."

When Sora hears this, she looks away in frustration and then leaves the room, punching the door with all her strength on the way out.

Daniel doesn't know what's wrong with her. When he's done with the doctor, he goes outside and finds her smoking a joint in the parking lot.

"What's wrong?" Daniel asks, cradling his stomach. "Why did you leave like that?"

Sora doesn't speak right away, taking a couple more drags from her joint before putting it out on the asphalt.

"I was hoping it wouldn't be a girl," she said.

"But a girl is safer than a boy," Daniel says. "She won't be at risk of being poisoned during the birth."

"Yeah, but I didn't want a girl."

"Why not?"

"Because it means she will be a scorpion. She's going to have to go through the same shit I went through when I was a child. She's going to have a rough life. I didn't want that for my child."

"But it won't be the same. She'll have a scorpion mother. You can help her. She won't have the same childhood you had. She won't go to the scorpion ranch."

She shakes her head. "I made a mistake. You should have had an abortion."

Daniel gets upset. "What? How can you say that?"

"It's not fair bringing a scorpion into this fucked up racist world."

"It's too late to be having second thoughts. I can't get an abortion now. We're having this baby no matter what."

Daniel goes to Sora and wraps his arms around her, pressing his swollen stomach against hers.

Sora says, "You know I'm right. You've been in that body long enough to know how hard it is to be like me. Everyone's going to hate that scorpion in your belly."

"Don't call her a scorpion," Daniel says, lying his head on her shoulder.

Sora touches Daniel on the top of his shoulder. But instead of embracing him, she pushes him away and goes back to the car.

The next day, Sora leaves Daniel without saying a word. She just leaves a note on the coffee table, taking only one bag and suitcase full of her personal things.

The note says:

> I'm sorry, Sora. I just can't do it. I can't marry you. I'm not ready to be a father. I know that I'm leaving a lot on you and I know that you don't deserve any of it. I'm just selfish. I've always been selfish. I was only with you because I wanted you to fill a hole in me that I thought needed

to be filled, but I now know that nothing is going to fill it. Not you. Not a child. Not a normal life. Because of my past, I'm just hollow inside. That hole is only going to get bigger and there's nothing I can do about it. You were the closest thing I've ever had to family, but it was all a fantasy. Deep down, we both know that it never would have worked out. I'm just not the kind of person who knows how to love. You probably won't think it's true, but I promise this is what's best for all of us. You're better off without me. The baby is better off without me. You'll be happier on your own. And I know you'll be a great mother. I'm sure you will hate me for leaving you in your current condition, robbing you of a future, stealing everything that was yours, but it's the only thing I can think of to do. I can't take the baby away from her mother. She needs you, not me. And she needs you the way you are. There's no turning back, for either of us. I'm sorry I took away your choice in the matter. I'm sure you'll never forgive me. I hope you and the baby are able to create a happy life together. Please don't try to find me. You'll never get back what you want even if you do.

Your ex-hubby,
Daniel Munch

After Daniel finishes reading the letter, he just stands there in shock. The note slips from his hands and falls on the floor as he stares forward. He can't believe she would do this to him.

She made him switch bodies with him. She got him pregnant. She forced him to carry the child. And now she just leaves him out of nowhere? She just took his body and ran, leaving him with nothing? As a scorpion, he can't take care of himself without her help. He can't get a job. He has no idea how to raise a child on his own. He's absolutely fucked.

Daniel believes his only option is to find Sora and get his body back. If she doesn't want to marry him, he's fine with that. If she doesn't want to raise their child, he won't blame her. But he needs to be himself again. He'll raise his daughter in his own body without Sora. But without his body, he won't be able to make money. He won't be able to provide for her. He can't let Sora get away with stealing his identity.

She drained both of their bank accounts, leaving him with nothing but the leftover cash he got from Jason. She took his car, his phone, and all of his identification. There's nothing he has that will prove who he is.

He goes to the police station and tells them everything about what happened to him. The officer tries to be patient with him, but really just wants the crazy scorpion chick to get the hell away from him as soon as possible.

"So you're saying that some scorpion bitch switched bodies with you and then took off with it? Right after she got you pregnant?"

"Yes, that's exactly what I'm saying!"

"Do you have any proof? What hospital did you do the switch in?"

Daniel hesitates for a moment, but decides to tell the truth.

"It wasn't at a hospital," he says. "It was in some warehouse. Sora said that it was under the table."

The cop rolls his eyes. "Well, if you're really saying that

you did a body swap on the black market then I'm supposed to arrest you. Not only that, but there's no proof that you actually switched bodies. If you had done the procedure legally there's protections against that kind of thing. You can't just steal somebody's body and get away with it. Records are created showing who is in what body. It's not easy to get away with unless you change your identity and move to another country. But on the black market, there's nothing you can do. She can just take over your life without any repercussions. She doesn't even have to change her identity. She's you now. And you're her. Legally, there's nothing anyone can do about it."

Daniel looks down at the floor, not sure how to respond to that.

The officer continues, "Sounds to me you got conned. Happens all the time. She was probably sick of being a scorpion and found some sad lonely guy to switch bodies with. You probably thought she loved you, am I right? That's what they always do. At least she didn't dump you with a body that's dying of cancer or one that's wanted for murder. When a murderer switches bodies with someone on the black market, we have no choice but to sentence the poor sap who got suckered into it. No way to prove he's innocent. Otherwise, all criminals would just claim they did a body swap. Our hands are tied."

"But what about the letter she wrote to me? Isn't that proof?"

He hands the cop the goodbye letter Sora left him.

As the officer reads the note, he just shakes his head and hands it back. "What does this prove? It just sounds like a guy ditching his pregnant girlfriend."

When he gets the note back, Daniel looks it over. He thought it was odd that she address the letter to Sora instead of Daniel. Now that he thinks about it, he realizes she was just trying to cover her tracks. She knew she was stealing his body so she left the note vague on purpose. She didn't want to leave any proof of the body swap. Nobody would believe that it's from a woman who stole his body.

Daniel still tries to convince him. "But I have witnesses, too. There's Tia, a friend of hers. And my boss. They both knew about our switch."

The cop doesn't want to hear it. "Look, I feel for you, I do. And I actually believe your story. I could write a report but it's not going to end well for you. Witnesses don't help in this sort of thing. Even if you could prove that you did a body swap, you'll just be arrested for doing an illegal procedure. The only thing I can recommend is to accept the fact that you're now this woman and sue your ex's ass for child support. Even though you're a scorpion now, the court will still side with you, maybe even more than a normal woman."

Daniel can't believe that is his only option. He knows there has to be another way.

"But how do I find her?" Daniel asks. "If I can find her then maybe I can convince her to give me her body back."

The cop shrugs. "I can't help you there. You might want to hire a private detective."

"I can't afford that."

"Well, that's the only option I can think of. Good luck."

The officer rushes him out of the office. Daniel isn't happy the police can't help him, but he understands. He wishes he never did the swap. He wishes he never met Sora. Although he's sure she didn't intentionally con him into giving her his body, he does believe that she knew exactly what she was doing when she stole his body out from under him. She would have covered her tracks, he's sure. He doubts he'll ever be able to find her unless she somehow has a change of heart and comes back to him.

Daniel tries calling his mother, hoping she will believe him despite the crazy story. He wishes he would have told her about doing the body swap, but he kept her in the dark on purpose. He knew that she hated the fact that he was dating a scorpion and would have been pissed if she knew he was engaged to her, let alone switching bodies with such a monster. If only he did that it would have been so much easier for him.

His mother won't listen to a word he says. He tries to tell her the whole story, but she thinks he's just some crazy bitch trying to fuck with her. Even when he tells her personal things about himself that only she would know about, she still doesn't believe him. She thinks he's just the scorpion girl who he's dating trying to cause problems. Daniel could have told a girlfriend all sorts of personal information about his childhood and his relationship with his mother, so he's not able to convince her.

He doesn't know what else to do, tears rolling down his cheeks.

Before she hangs up on him, he says, "You'll know I'm telling the truth if you ever see her in my body. I doubt she'll ever go to you, but if you ever find her you'll know. She's not me. She looks like me, but she's nothing like me. You'll believe me then."

But his mother just says, "Don't ever call me again."

He can hear her crying as she cancels the call. For a second, he thinks he must have upset her by being so forceful with his voice. But then he wonders if he actually did convince her that he was telling the truth. His mother hates scorpions. She always has. Maybe she knew it really was Daniel and told him not to call her again because she didn't want to have anything to do with him now that he's in a scorpion's body. But maybe he's just being paranoid. She would never really do that. She might not want him over to her house anymore, but she would still want to talk to him, even in another person's body. No, she just didn't believe him. She refused to believe him. It's the only thing she could do to keep her sanity as a mother.

Daniel finds himself on Tia's doorstep one night. He doesn't know who else to go to. He has no idea where else to turn. When she opens the door, he just breaks down into tears. She invites him in and he tells her everything.

When he finishes his story, Tia looks at him with warm, comforting eyes. "I'm so sorry, Daniel. That's really fucked up. Even for Sora."

"I don't know what I'm going to do," he says, wiping his tears away. "She stole my body. She left me alone and pregnant. I don't know how I'm going to make money. The police can't help me. My parents won't talk to me. I'm completely fucked."

Tia doesn't say anything. She just wraps her arms around him and holds him close to her. She hugs him so tightly that his breasts hurt while being squished against hers. But despite the awkwardness, he finds himself leaning into her hug. He rests his head on her shoulder and just lets his tears fall. He's never felt more comfortable in another person's embrace in a very long time.

He stays there for a while, crying against Tia's chest.

Then she says, "You don't have to worry about a thing. I'm here for you. I'll help you."

He doesn't believe her, but her words are exactly what he needed to hear. She's a weird girl that he's been sleeping with just to make his fiancé feel better about her own infidelity. He doesn't really like her that much. He's not that attracted to her and only thinks of her as a friend for helping him through his pregnancy, but right now she's the most important thing in the world to him.

She releases her embrace and looks him in the eyes. "I love you, Daniel. I love you even more than I loved Sora. Maybe your body was stolen for a reason. Maybe it's what had to happen in order for you to find me. I want to take care of you. I want to help you raise your baby. Will you move in with me?"

Daniel tenses up. She just said the craziest, most awkward thing anyone has ever said to him in his life. But for some reason, he finds himself nodding his head and returning to her embrace. He needs somebody, anybody, to show him the kind of warmth he wishes he would've gotten from Sora. He needs help. He'd rather die than go through this alone.

Tia strokes his hair and kisses his forehead.

"I'll make you happy," she tells him. "I promise you I'll make you the happiest woman in the world."

CHAPTER
ELEVEN

Daniel moves in with Tia. It's only a small studio apartment, but at least it's a lot cheaper than his old place. If they split the cost it would be less than a quarter of what he'd have to pay for his old apartment, but she's not asking him for any money. He sells most of his belongings and all of the stuff Sora left behind. Her manga collection goes for quite a bit of money. Daniel thinks he can get by for most his pregnancy on just that money alone. But Tia wants to take care of him. She tells him that he should save all of his money for after the baby is born. She wants to keep him happy so that he will stay with her, forever. Like Sora, she's had a lonely life as a scorpion. She needs somebody to fill the hole in her that nothing has been able to fill before.

Of all the people he's ever been with, Tia is the one who makes him feel the most loved. She really showers him with affection and puts everything she has into their relationship. Daniel knows that she really thinks of him as Sora. She even stopped referring to him as Daniel and now addresses him as Sora and only Sora.

"It's your name now," she says. "You're not Daniel anymore. You should just accept it."

Daniel knows that Tia wants him to become Sora for her. She wants him to accept that identity so that she can finally have Sora all to herself. She admitted that Sora is the only one she's ever truly loved even though she knew they were never meant to be. But now she has a new Sora in her life and she has a shot with her. This Sora is the one who was meant to be her true soul mate. And now that she has her she plans to never let her go.

He feels bad for taking advantage of this woman, but he needs her help. Nobody else would ever want anything to do with a scorpion like him. Nobody else will give a shit about the fact that he's pregnant and isn't able to get a job.

Tia does cam work for a living. She isn't very popular, but she has an OnlyFans page and works for a bunch of different websites. She specializes in doing all sorts of things that other scorpion cam girls aren't willing to do, like fart fetish videos and extreme insertion. She can stick a whole bottle of champagne into her rectum backwards and then pour it into a glass and drink it. She also does a bunch of poison ejaculation videos, but that's mostly because she can't orgasm without discharging her venom.

Daniel agrees to do some videos with her. As a pregnant scorpion, he's able to get a lot of attention. It's a pretty rare thing to find, despite how many scorpions are doing sex work on the internet these days. Having lesbian sex live on a stream is not something Daniel ever saw himself doing with his life, but it's not bad work. It's far more fun than the sets he did with that Jason creep. At least he feels safe and in control of the situation. They give each other oral and squish their boobs together and rub Daniel's swollen stomach and drink the venom from each other's vaginas and smile at the camera while squirting milk from Daniel's lactating breasts. It's really easy work for the most part and Tia's page has been getting more popular than ever because of him.

Daniel is thinking about starting his own page. All of the promotion and behind the scenes work seems like too much of a pain, but Tia says she'll do all that for him. All he needs to do is the videos and interact with people online. He agrees only because he thinks it will piss Sora off if she ever finds him using her body to do work that she's given up a long time ago.

He hopes that Sora is having just as hard of a time adapting to life in his body as he is in hers. She can't do her old jobs as Daniel. She has to figure out something new she can do. If she goes back to Daniel's old job and tells them she dumped the scorpion she was with, she'd surely be able to get rehired. But she has no idea how to do the work he used to do, just as much as he doesn't know how to do any of the computer work she made a living doing. Both of them have to start over from scratch. Deep down, he knows she'll have no problem finding her footing. But he likes the idea of thinking about her struggling with it. He wants her to regret leaving him. He knows it's petty, but he thinks she deserves all the hardship the world can possibly throw at her.

When Daniel gives birth, Tia stays by his side. She holds his hand the whole time, telling him how beautiful his child will be. He doesn't tell her how thankful he is to have her with him, but he's sure she can tell by the way he presses his sweaty face against her arm and kisses her hand.

The pain is far worse than he could have possibly imagined. He knew it would be bad, but nobody ever told him it would be as bad as this. He has a narrow pelvis, so the doctor has difficulty pulling the baby out. It gets stuck. The doctor has to break her arm in order to pull the child out.

"It'll heal," Tia tells him. "Don't worry about it. Babies heal quickly."

When the baby is finally out of him, Daniel sees the little creature with bright blue skin, red arms and legs, and little black hands and feet that make her look like she's wearing gloves and socks.

"Oh my god…" Tia says, beginning to cry. "She's so precious."

The doctor gives the baby to Daniel and he holds her in his arms. He feels so awkward holding it. The thought of becoming a mother is only just now sinking in. He's not just stuck being a woman, he's also a mother who has a child to look after. He knows his whole life is about to change forever. It's all been such a whirlwind of crazy events since he met Sora, all leading up to this moment.

He always hoped he would be a parent one day. He just never knew this was the kind of parent he would become.

Daniel can't believe he has a baby now. He stares down at her as she suckles on his dark blue nipple, drinking his milk that he still has no idea how the hell his body is able to produce. Her tiny eyes are squeezed shut and her big blue cheeks seem to twinkle in the light.

He never thought of what to name her when he was pregnant. He really never thought he'd actually have to give birth to her, thinking somehow, for some reason, Sora would return and give him his body back. He didn't even think of the baby as completely his. Like his body, he saw the baby as Sora's. He was just carrying her child for her, borrowing her body until she reclaimed it. But now that the child is born, he doesn't want to give it up, he doesn't want to give her body back. This child isn't Sora's. It's his. He gave birth to her. Sora can never take her away from him.

He wants to name her Wrinkly because of all the cute wrinkles in her face. But he decides that it would mess her up too much. Instead, he decides Winnie would be a better name.

"What is Winnie short for?" Tia asks him.

Daniel shrugs. "I don't know. Maybe Winter?"

"Yeah, I like Winter," Tia says.

Tia holds out her hands. "Can I hold her?"

Daniel nods and lifts the baby to her. "Be careful. Hold her head."

Tia lifts the child up and smiles wide, staring into the baby's face with her crazy eyes, "Hello, Winnie! I'm your second mommy. I'm so happy to meet you."

Daniel thinks it's a little weird that Tia would call herself Winter's second mommy, but he's not too upset about it. If Tia gets connected to his daughter that will only help him in the long run. She will be there for the baby when he needs help. Maybe she will even help him raise her. He can't do it on his own. He's not even able to get by on his own without her help. She can be his daughter's second mother if she wants to be. Tia is an oddball but she'd make a great second mom.

His first year of being a mother is pretty rough on Daniel. The three of them trapped in that tiny apartment with a screaming baby nearly causes him to break. The lack of sleep, the diapers, the pain in his nipples from all the breastfeeding. The only thing that keeps him going is Tia's positive attitude. She's been happier than she's ever been in her life since Winter was born. It's like she really is Winnie's second mother, showing her just as much love as if she was her own daughter. Tia's been an absolute godsend. Daniel thanks the stars that he has her in his life. He wouldn't have been able to do it without her. She's not Sora, but she's the perfect person for him at this moment in his life.

Daniel doesn't do any cam girl work anymore. He has to

take Winter out of the house for a walk whenever Tia needs to do a stream, giving her privacy so that she can moan as loud as she can without waking Winter or having a crying baby in the background. They aren't making as much money as they were before, but they have enough savings to get by. Daniel plans to try to get a remote job doing accounting work at some point. He's going to take a page out of Sora's handbook and lie on his application. He has the experience but he has no way to prove it. Lying is the only way to get a job that he's actually qualified for.

Tia and Daniel get married when Winnie turns two. They don't have a wedding. They don't have enough close friends or family that would show up anyway. They get a babysitter, the only one in town willing to watch scorpion kids, so that they can go on a honeymoon to Vegas for a few nights.

Daniel decides he no longer wants to go by his old name anymore. Tia stopped calling him that ages ago anyway. He's now Sora. He isn't the man he used to be. He's a scorpion now. And, for the sake of his daughter, he has to be proud of who he is from now on. He's erasing everything that happened to him leading up to Winter's birth, throwing away all of his memories of himself as a man. He's now Sora. A scorpion. A mother to the most beautiful little girl he's ever seen in his life.

And Sora doesn't need the past she had before. Sora has a future. She's looking forward to it with bated breath. She has a partner who cares about her. She does work that she finds fun and rewarding. She's saving up money and keeping in good shape. She's building the right confidence she needs to raise a child in a world that wants nothing to do with either of them.

After four years of living in a tiny studio apartment, Sora finally moves out. She buys a house on the outskirts of town and moves there with her wife and their daughter. The house is really old, built in 1908, and has probably been flooded and burned down and rebuilt many times over the years. It's not very large. Just a two bedroom, one bath. But it has a lot of land, so much that she can't see their neighbor's house or anyone else that lives on their quiet country road. Nobody in the neighborhood even knows that a group of scorpions live here.

They call their home the scorpion ranch. Tia named it that as a joke. Her dream is to turn it into some kind of ranch at some point. Maybe a horse ranch or even an ostrich ranch. Whatever it is, it will be the only ranch in the country owned and operated by three scorpion women. But Sora knows Tia's dreams aren't really anything she takes seriously. She just wants Winnie to have a safe and happy childhood.

There's another scorpion couple within driving distance that have a child that's Winnie's age. Even though her parents pass as human, their daughter is brightly colored with black, blue and red skin. She looks so similar to Winnie that the two could be sisters. And when they go out together, everyone always assumes that Sora is their mom. The four adults agree that they want their children to grow up together. Even if they have no one else in the world who understands them, at least they will have each other.

Not having to face much bigotry, Winter grows up like any normal kid and doesn't seem to realize how different she is. She doesn't think it's odd that there aren't many people who look like her on television. In fact, she feels sorry for anyone who doesn't have the same colors as she does.

They get a pitbull puppy for Winnie on her sixth birthday and name him Destro. Sora thinks it'll be a good protector for her when it grows up, a dog that will scare the neighbors away. But the puppy is so adorable that Tia says there's no way anyone could ever be scared of such a friendly animal.

Winnie is playing with Destro in the field in front of the house while Tia and Sora are sitting on the porch, keeping an eye on her while cooking teriyaki chicken on the charcoal grill. A car pulls up in the driveway. It moves slowly, cautiously, the driver getting a good look at the little scorpion girl running through the weeds.

Sora gets to her feet, staring down the driver. She knows this person is going to be trouble. Something about the way he moves forward with determination, running over Winnie's toys that she left on the dirt trail leading up to the house, makes her think she needs to be on high alert.

"Get Winter and take her inside," Sora tells her wife.

Tia doesn't hesitate. She calls Winnie and Destro over and they go inside, locking the door behind them. There's a shotgun under the bed. Tia knows the drill. She gets the gun and puts herself between Winnie and the front door.

Sora picks up a shovel from the side of the house and rests it on her shoulder. She walks toward the car with the most intimidating posture she can muster.

The car stops and a man steps out. Sora's jaw drops open when she sees him. He's the last person that she'd ever expect showing up on her doorstep.

"What are you going to do with that?" Daniel says, as he takes off his sunglasses and steps toward her.

"Daniel?" she asks.

He's amused that she would call him by that name.

He smirks at her and says, "It's good to see you, Sora. Been a long time."

"What the fuck are you doing here?" she asks, lowering

the shovel. She doesn't put it down, though. A part of her still wants to hit him with it.

"It took forever to track you down. I wanted to see you."

"About what? Do you want your body back or something?"

He shakes his head. "No, no. I'm sorry, but I've adjusted to this body a little too well to give it up. I hope you don't hate me for it."

She always fantasized about tracking Daniel down again. She had so many things she wanted to say to him, so many things she wanted to *do* to him. But now that he's finally in front of her, all of those words have escaped her.

"Then what did you come here for?" she asks.

"I've come to see my daughter," Daniel says.

"You already saw her. Now you can go."

Daniel gets annoyed that she would turn him away so quickly.

"I've come a long way. I live in Texas now. I'm here on business. I'm not sure when I'll be able to come out this way again."

Sora really doesn't care about inconveniencing him. She doesn't want him to take another step forward.

"Was that Tia I saw in there?" he asks, nodding toward the house. Sora looks back to see her wife staring at them through the window. "I'm happy you two hit it off. She's a sweet girl. I knew she'd make you happy."

Sora doesn't want to hear it. Her face twists up in anger, no longer able to hold back her emotions. "How could you fucking leave me like that? Do you know what I had to go through because of you?"

He tries to express compassion, but it only comes across as fake. There's something about him that just makes her sick. He just seems like a self-absorbed douchebag, the kind of guy she always hated.

"I know. I'm an asshole. Saying I'm sorry will never be enough."

"What have you been doing with my body all these years?"

Daniel shrugs. "You know, just taking it a day at a time. I traveled around quite a bit for the first few years. But then I met a woman and settled down. We're getting married in the spring. I know you don't care, but I'm happy. I'm really happy."

"Have you reached out to my parents?"

Daniel shakes his head. "No, I couldn't do that. I ran into some friends of yours in New York a while back and tried to play it off like I remembered them, but I think they knew something was wrong. I took off before they could ask me any more questions."

Sora tries to think about who he might be talking about, but she just lets it go. She hasn't spoken to any of her friends in so long, even before she moved away from her hometown. She doesn't really care about them anymore. She knows that all of her old friends were really prejudiced against scorpions and would never want anything to do with her now. Though it would have been nice if they were able to out Daniel as a fake and let her parents know. She wants them to feel guilty for not listening to her when she was in her moment of need.

"You really fucked me," Sora says to him, her eyes searing with hate.

He nods. "I know. I get it. Just let me see our daughter and I'll be on my way. Just give me fifteen minutes."

"Fuck that. I won't even give you fifteen seconds with her."

Daniel loses his patience. "Come on. Don't be such a bitch."

"Are you seriously calling me a bitch after what you did?"

"You don't have to punish our daughter just because you hate me. She deserves to meet her father."

"You're not her father!" Sora screams. "You're not anything to her and you never will be."

He kicks the ground, his face turning red. "What the fuck, Sora? Why are you being such a cunt? I was never like that when I was you."

"Oh, you were way worse. You were always a self-absorbed piece of shit."

Daniel points at her. "That's not true and you know it."

"Just get the fuck out of here," Sora says, gripping her shovel tighter. "I don't want to ever see your ugly face ever again."

Daniel laughs out loud. "It was your face first."

"Go! I don't care. Get the fuck out. Now."

Daniel holds his ground. "Not until I see my daughter."

Sora doesn't say anything. She just sucks poison out of her venom gland and spits it at his shoes.

"What the fuck, Sora?" he cries, trying to kick the poison off of his shoe. "That's dangerous!"

Sora takes a step forward. "I'm going to aim at your face next."

"Are you serious?" he yells.

"Dead serious."

Daniel doesn't leave right away. He takes a step back and huffs and puffs, kicking the wheels of his car. Then he turns back and says, "Fine. I was just being nice anyway. Fuck you. Fuck all three of you scorpion cunts."

Then he gets back into his car and revs the engine as loud as he can. He tears out across the dirt road, spraying rocks across the porch as he zooms backwards out of the property.

Before he gets to the main road, Daniel rolls down the window and pokes his head out. "Have fun with your miserable life!"

Then he speeds off.

Tia rushes out of the house as Sora breaks down into tears, wrapping her arms around her, still holding the shotgun tightly in her yellow fingers.

Sora wipes her eyes and goes back to the grill, pulling off all the burned chicken.

"I'll order a pizza," Tia says, returning to the house.

While Sora tries to collect herself, Winter comes up behind her, carrying her favorite stuffed frog they got from the zoo, the poison dart frog that has the same patterns in its skin as she and her mother have.

"Was that my daddy?" Winter asks.

Sora doesn't look at her. She shakes her head and tries to bury her emotions. "No, it wasn't."

Winter looks at the empty road and then back at her mother.

"Who is my daddy?" the girl asks.

Sora turns to her, looking into her black wet innocent eyes. "I am," Sora tells her.

Then she picks her daughter up and carries her back into the house.

Sora knows that someday she'll have to tell her daughter the whole story, but that won't be for a very long time. She doesn't want Winter to have to deal with that kind of information. Her daughter doesn't understand stuff like body swaps or venomous women or even how babies are made.

She wants Winter to hold onto her innocence for as long as possible, because this world is one big motherfucker that's full of horrible people who don't give a fuck about anyone else but themselves. It is full of people who feel justified for being assholes, who are always coming up with reasons to put other people down. Even those who consider themselves good people, who think their morals are without flaw and absolutely in the right, don't realize how much damage they cause to so many others around them.

And if Sora can protect her daughter from them, even for a little while, then maybe she won't turn out quite as damaged as the rest of us.

BONUS SECTION

This is the part of the book where we would have published an afterword by the author but he insisted on drawing a comic strip instead for reasons we don't quite understand.

Thank you for reading my new book, *Scorpion Ranch,* I hope you enjoyed it!

It's me CM3!

When I started writing this book, I decided to call it Scorpion Ranch because I always wanted to write a book with that title.

It's been sitting in my big list of story titles for many years now.

I keep a journal and there are hundreds if not thousands of titles for stories I may or may never write.

Originally, I was going to use the title for a memoir I was going to write about my childhood.

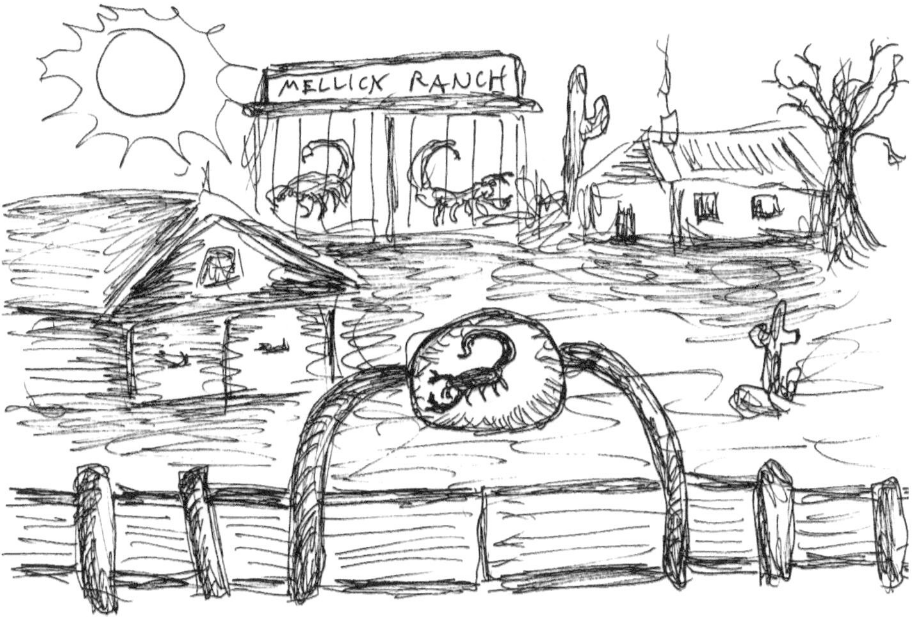

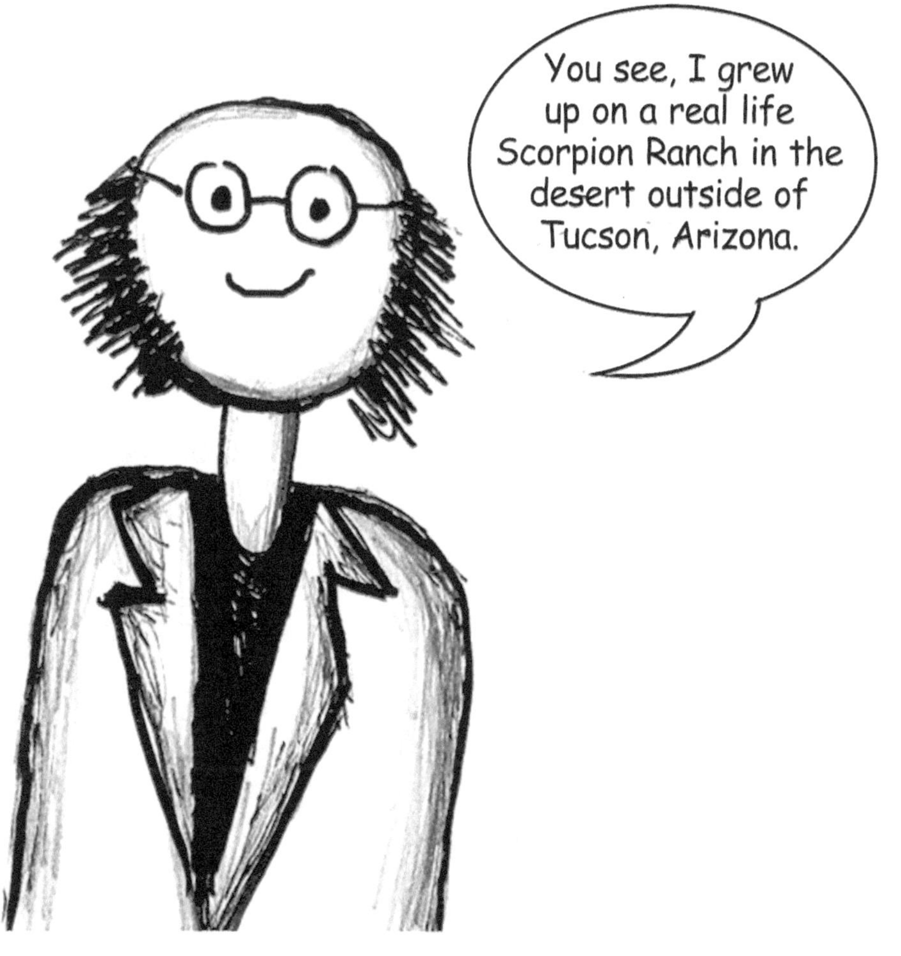

My parents were scorpion ranchers.

They used to raise giant scorpions for a living.

If you ever purchased scorpion steaks or gallons of scorpion milk from your local grocery store back in the 1980s, there's a good chance that they came from my parents' scorpion ranch.

Scorpion MILK
$1.75 each

MILK MILK MILK MILK

Scorpion Steaks
79¢ a pound

MELLICK RANCH

During those years, I loved going scorpionback riding in the desert behind my house.

Or watching the scorpions climb up the side of the barn at night to shoot lasers at the owls.

It was a pretty good business for several years until one of the scorpions got loose and found its way into the nearby daycare center.

I guess it ate a bunch of toddlers or something. The whole town was really upset with my parents after that.

To pay off all the settlements, we had to sell the rest of our scorpions to the military.

I believe they were used in Operation Desert Storm in 1991.

I'm not sure what happened to them, but I like to think our scorpions became national heroes.

Those were fond childhood memories.

They make me nostalgic just thinking about them.

But I guess I'll never write that book now. When I started writing this one, I came up with the idea of calling the venomous women "scorpions" and I just didn't have any other book title ideas with the word scorpion in it. So this book became Scorpion Ranch and I'll never write the other one.

Oh well, I'll never live long enough to write all the thousands of books I want to write so I have to pick and choose and abandon some here and there.

It's the curse of being a writer.

That and the systematic oppression of the self employed in this country.

THE
END

PS – this actually was going to be a real novel I planned to write. I'm kind of sad I'll never get to write it.

ABOUT THE AUTHOR

Carlton Mellick III has made a living writing bizarro fiction novels to a cult audience for over twenty years. He was named one of the top forty genre fiction authors under the age of forty by the guardian. His work has been translated into German, Spanish, Italian, Czech, Polish, Russian, Turkish, Persian, French and Japanese.

He lives on the Washington Coast with his wife, Rose, and his pet water spider, Yuki.

Visit him online at **www.carltonmellick.com**

STACKING DOLL

Benjamin never thought he'd ever fall in love with anyone, let alone a Matryoshkan, but from the moment he met Ynaria he knew she was the only one for him. Although relationships between humans and Matryoshkans are practically unheard of, the two are determined to get married despite objections from their friends and family. After meeting Ynaria's strict conservative parents, it becomes clear to Benjamin that the only way they will approve of their union is if they undergo The Trial—a matryoshkan wedding tradition where couples lock themselves in a house for several days in order to introduce each other to all of the people living inside of them.

SNUGGLE CLUB

After the death of his wife, Ray Parker decides to get involved with the local "cuddle party" community in order to once again feel the closeness of another human being. Although he's sure it will be a strange and awkward experience, he's determined to give anything a try if it will help him overcome his crippling loneliness. But he has no idea just how unsettling of an experience it will be until it's far too late to escape.

MOUSE TRAP

It's the last school trip young Emily will ever get to go on. Not because it's the end of the school year, but because the world is coming to an end. Teachers, parents, and other students have been slowly dying off over the past several months, killed in mysterious traps that have been appearing across the countryside. Nobody knows where the traps come from or who put them there, but they seem to be designed to exterminate the entirety of the human race.

Emily thought it was going to be an ordinary trip to the local amusement park, but what was supposed to be a normal afternoon of bumper cars and roller coasters has turned into a fight for survival after their teacher is horrifically killed in front of them, leaving the small children to fend for themselves in a life or death game of mouse and mouse trap.

WHY I MARRIED A CLOWN GIRL FROM THE DIMENSION OF DEATH

Timothy is terrified of clowns. He's always found them disturbing and creepy and weird. But now that our world is besieged by clown-like invaders from another dimension, his phobia is spiraling out of control. Timothy has no idea how to handle living in a world full of these cartoonish creatures until he meets a clown girl named Puppy Caterpillars who happens to be the cutest, sweetest girl he's ever encountered. They fall in love and Timothy believes his phobia has finally been cured. But after they get married, Timothy discovers his phobia might have been the only thing keeping him alive.

GLASS CHILDREN

The children of the glass generation are the most sensitive, fragile, entitled, spoiled, lazy, selfish little brats that human society has ever produced. Part of this is due to overprotective parenting, but it is mostly due to the fact that these children are literally made out of glass. Nobody knows why, but one day the human species went through a surreal mutation where babies started being born with delicate hollow glass bodies with no flesh or bones or anything holding them together but their thin delicate exoskeleton.

YOU ALWAYS TRY TO KILL ME IN YOUR DREAMS

Dreams shouldn't kill you. If you die in a dream you should be fine in real life. But that's not what Elias learns once he moves in with a girl named Roe who has the terrible habit of pulling people into her dreams with her whenever she falls asleep. Although she's the nicest, coolest, most attractive woman Elias has ever known while she's awake, Roe is a complete psychopath in her dreams. She will stop at nothing to kill anyone who finds their way into her subconscious worlds. But Elias has no choice but to survive her crazy dreams every night if he ever hopes to make it in a world that has been torn apart by a global pandemic and economic collapse.

APESHIP

An intolerable prick takes his weird daughter, his college-aged girlfriend, her douchey brother and her awkward best friend on a boating trip to show off his new yacht. But when they come across an abandoned cruise ship in the middle of the ocean, they find themselves hunted by a group of sadistic mutant killers hell-bent on keeping them as their immortal playthings for all eternity.

THE GIRL WITH THE BARBED WIRE HAIR

There is a girl who lives in the alley behind the old, abandoned fire station. She is always covered in ash and grime, cuts and bruises on her arms and legs, the skirt of her school uniform caked in dirt and ripped into tatters. Her hair is a mess of dreadlocks the color of rusted metal, growing like vines all the way down to her ankles. She was once human, but not anymore. She's become a feral creature with an undying thirst for blood and revenge. But when she meets a young boy named Yusuke, the first person to ever show her an ounce of human kindness, her desire for revenge turns to feelings of love. And she will do whatever it takes to win his heart, even if she has to rip it from his chest in order to obtain it.

SCORPION RANCH

Daniel Munch is in a toxic relationship, but not just because his girlfriend is selfish and manipulative. She is also literally toxic—born with glands in her mouth and genitals that spew deadly poison. Every time they kiss or make love, he puts his life at risk. She could kill him at any moment and he has no choice but to trust that she would never do anything to cause him harm. But when they decide to get married, Daniel is pressured into doing *the switch*—a procedure where couples swap bodies in order to better understand each other. For one month, he will become her girlfriend while she will become his boyfriend. It's only for one month, so what would be the harm in giving it a shot? Surely it wouldn't utterly destroy each and every aspect of his entire life…

GOBLINS ON THE OTHER SIDE

There are no mistakes in Heaven. There are no flaws, no worries, no ugliness. Everything is perfect. Everyone is nice to each other and happy all of the time. Nobody is selfish or spiteful or mean. It is a place of peace and harmony. A place of love and hope and friendship. Nothing bad ever happens there. But if you plan to visit, be sure to follow all of the rules. Stay inside your family's designated area at all times. Do not venture off the beaten path. Always wear your goblin mask when looking out of the windows. And, most importantly, refrain from thinking unhappy thoughts. Negativity in Heaven is prohibited.

FULL METAL OCTOPUS

Eliot is the most beautiful fairy in all of the city with his dazzling emerald green butterfly wings that make everyone who sees them fall instantly in lust with him. But it's more of a curse than a blessing. Forced to hide his wings in public in order to avoid the constant sexual harassment, Eliot only finds solace when visiting his friends at the Snake Pit lamia strip club or getting tattooed by the dark and mysterious half-octopus woman named Oona.

THE BAD BOX

Little Benny isn't very good at taking tests. It's not that he's a stupid kid or doesn't pay attention in class. It's just that he's absolutely terrified of failure. It doesn't matter how hard he studies. He gets so nervous that he freezes up and his mind goes blank, rarely even answering a single question before the time is up. This is especially difficult now that he's in Mrs. Gustafson's fifth grade class, where the punishment for failure is to draw a curse from the bad box—a magical device that permanently mutates children into horrific monsters.

BIO MELT

Nobody goes into the Wire District anymore. The place is an industrial wasteland of poisonous gas clouds and lakes of toxic sludge. The machines are still running, the drone-operated factories are still spewing biochemical fumes over the city, but the place has lain abandoned for decades.

When the area becomes flooded by a mysterious black ooze, six strangers find themselves trapped in the Wire District with no chance of escape or rescue. Banding together, they must find a way through the sea of bio-waste before the deadly atmosphere wipes them out. But there are dark things growing within the toxic slime around them, grotesque mutant creatures that have long been forgotten by the rest of civilization. They are known only as clusters--colossal monstrosities made from the fused-together body parts of a thousand discarded clones. They are lost, frightened, and very, very hungry.

THE TERRIBLE THING THAT HAPPENS

There is a grocery store. The last grocery store in the world. It stands alone in the middle of a vast wasteland that was once our world. The open sign is still illuminated, brightening the black landscape. It can be seen from miles away, even through the poisonous red ash. Every night at the exact same time, the store comes alive. It becomes exactly as it was before the world ended. Its shelves are replenished with fresh food and water. Ghostly shoppers walk the aisles. The scent of freshly baked breads can be smelled from the rust-caked parking lot. For generations, a small community of survivors, hideously mutated from the toxic atmosphere, have survived by collecting goods from the store. But it is not an easy task. Decades ago, before the world was destroyed, there was a terrible thing that happened in this place. A group of armed men in brown paper masks descended on the shopping center, massacring everyone in sight. This horrible event reoccurs every night, in the exact same manner. And the only way the wastelanders can gather enough food for their survival is to traverse the killing spree, memorize the patterns, and pray they can escape the bloodbath in tact.

THE BIG MEAT

In the center of the city once known as Portland, Oregon, there lies a mountain of flesh. Hundreds of thousands of tons of rotting flesh. It has filled the city with disease and dead-lizard stench, contaminated the water supply with its greasy putrid fluids, clogged the air with toxic gasses so thick that you can't leave your house without the aid of a gas mask. And no one really knows quite what to do about it. A thousand-man demolition crew has been trying to clear it out one piece at a time, but after three months of work they've barely made a dent. And then there's the junkies who have started burrowing into the monster's guts, searching for a drug produced by its fire glands, setting back the excavation even longer.

It seems like the corpse will never go away. And with the quarantine still in place, we're not even allowed to leave. We're stuck in this disgusting rotten hell forever.

EVER TIME WE MEET AT THE DAIRY QUEEN, YOUR WHOLE FUCKING FACE EXPLODES

Ethan is in love with the weird girl in school. The one with the twitchy eyes and spiders in her hair. The one who can't sit still for even a minute and speaks in an odd squeaky voice. The one they call Spiderweb.

Although she scares all the other kids in school, Ethan thinks Spiderweb is the cutest, sweetest, most perfect girl in the world. But there's a problem. Whenever they go on a date at the Dairy Queen, her whole fucking face explodes. He's not sure why it happens. She just gets so excited that pressure builds under her skin. Then her face bursts, spraying meat and gore across the room, her eyeballs and lips landing in his strawberry sundae.

At first, Ethan believes he can deal with his girlfriend's face-exploding condition. But the more he gets to know her, the weirder her condition turns out to be. And as their relationship gets serious, Ethan realizes that the only way to make it work is to become just as strange as she is.

EXERCISE BIKE

There is something wrong with Tori Manetti's new exercise bike. It is made from flesh and bone. It eats and breathes and poops. It was once a billionaire named Darren Oscarson who underwent years of cosmetic surgery to be transformed into a human exercise bike so that he could live out his deepest sexual fantasy. Now Tori is forced to ride him, use him as a normal piece of exercise equipment, no matter how grotesque his appearance.

SPIDER BUNNY

Only Petey remembers the Fruit Fun cereal commercials of the 1980s. He remembers how warped and disturbing they were. He remembers the lumpy-shaped cartoon children sitting around a breakfast table, eating puffy pink cereal brought to them by the distortedly animated mascot, Berry Bunny. The characters were creepier than the Sesame Street Humpty Dumpty, freakier than Mr. Noseybonk from the old BBC show Jigsaw. They used to give him nightmares as a child. Nightmares where Berry Bunny would reach out of the television and grab him, pulling him into her cereal bowl to be eaten by the demented cartoon children.

When Petey brings up Fruit Fun to his friends, none of them have any idea what he's talking about. They've never heard of the cereal or seen the commercials before. And they're not the only ones. Nobody has ever heard of it. There's not even any information about Fruit Fun on google or wikipedia. At first, Petey thinks he's going crazy. He wonders if all of those commercials were real or just false memories. But then he starts seeing them again. Berry Bunny appears on his television, promoting Fruit Fun cereal in her squeaky unsettling voice. And the next thing Petey knows, he and his friends are sucked into the cereal commercial and forced to survive in a surreal world populated by cartoon characters made flesh.

NEVERDAY

Karl Lybeck has been repeating the same day over and over again, in a constant loop, for what feels like a thousand years. He thought he was the only person trapped in this eternal hell until he meets a young woman named January who is trapped in the same loop that Karl's been stuck within for so many centuries. But it turns out that Karl and January aren't alone. In fact, the majority of the population has been repeating the same day just as they have been. And society has mutated into something completely different from the world they once knew.

THE BOY WITH THE CHAINSAW HEART

Mark Knight awakens in the afterlife and discovers that he's been drafted into Hell's army, forced to fight against the hordes of murderous angels attacking from the North. He finds himself to be both the pilot and the fuel of a demonic war machine known as Lynx, a living demon woman with the ability to mutate into a weaponized battle suit that reflects the unique destructive force of a man's soul.

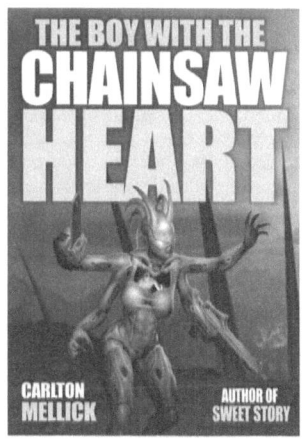

PARASITE MILK

Irving Rice has just arrived on the planet Kynaria to film an episode of the popular Travel Channel television series *Bizarre Foods with Andrew Zimmern: Intergalactic Edition*. Having never left his home state, let alone his home planet, Irving is hit with a severe case of culture shock. He's not prepared for Kynaria's mushroom cities, fungus-like citizens, or the giant insect wildlife. He's also not prepared for the consequences after he spends the night with a beautiful nymph-like alien woman who infects Irving with dangerous sexually-transmitted parasites that turn his otherworldly business trip into an agonizing fight for survival.

CUDDLY HOLOCAUST

Teddy bears, dollies, and little green soldiers—they've all had enough of you. They're sick of being treated like playthings for spoiled little brats. They have no rights, no property, no hope for a future of any kind. You've left them with no other option-in order to be free, they must exterminate the human race.

Julie is a human girl undergoing reconstructive surgery in order to become a stuffed animal. Her plan: to infiltrate enemy lines in order to save her family from the toy death camps. But when an army of plushy soldiers invade the underground bunker where she has taken refuge, Julie will be forced to move forward with her plan despite her transformation being not entirely complete.

ARMADILLO FISTS

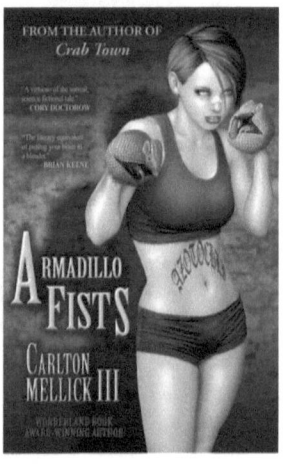

A weird-as-hell gangster story set in a world where people drive giant mechanical dinosaurs instead of cars.

Her name is Psycho June Howard, aka Armadillo Fists, a woman who replaced both of her hands with living armadillos. She was once the most bloodthirsty fighter in the world of illegal underground boxing. But now she is on the run from a group of psychotic gangsters who believe she's responsible for the death of their boss. With the help of a stegosaurus driver named Mr. Fast Awesome—who thinks he is God's gift to women even though he doesn't have any arms or legs--June must do whatever it takes to escape her pursuers, even if she has to kill each and every one of them in the process.

VILLAGE OF THE MERMAIDS

Mermaids are protected by the government under the Endangered Species Act, which means you aren't able to kill them even in self-defense. This is especially problematic if you happen to live in the isolated fishing village of Siren Cove, where there exists a healthy population of mermaids in the surrounding waters that view you as the main source of protein in their diet.

The only thing keeping these ravenous sea women at bay is the equally-dangerous supply of human livestock known as Food People. Normally, these "feeder humans" are enough to keep the mermaid population happy and well-fed. But in Siren Cove, the mermaids are avoiding the human livestock and have returned to hunting the frightened local fishermen. It is up to Doctor Black, an eccentric representative of the Food People Corporation, to investigate the matter and hopefully find a way to correct the mermaids' new eating patterns before the remaining villagers end up as fish food. But the more he digs, the more he discovers there are far stranger and more dangerous things than mermaids hidden in this ancient village by the sea.

I KNOCKED UP SATAN'S DAUGHTER

Jonathan Vandervoo lives a carefree life in a house made of legos, spending his days building lego sculptures and his nights getting drunk with his only friend—an alcoholic sumo wrestler named Shoji. It's a pleasant life with no responsibility, until the day he meets Lici. She's a soul-sucking demon from hell with red skin, glowing eyes, a forked tongue, and pointy red devil horns... and she claims to be nine months pregnant with Jonathan's baby.

Now Jonathan must do the right thing and marry the succubus or else her demonic family is going to rip his heart out through his ribcage and force him to endure the worst torture hell has to offer for the rest of eternity. But can Jonathan really love a fire-breathing, frog-eating, cold-blooded demoness? Or would eternal damnation be preferable? Either way, the big day is approaching. And once Jonathan's conservative Christian family learns their son is about to marry a spawn of Satan, it's going to be all-out war between demons and humans, with Jonathan and his hell-born bride caught in the middle.

KILL BALL

In a city where everyone lives inside of plastic bubbles, there is no such thing as intimacy. A husband can no longer kiss his wife. A mother can no longer hug her children. To do this would mean instant death. Ever since the disease swept across the globe, we have become isolated within our own personal plastic prison cells, rolling aimlessly through rubber streets in what are essentially man-sized hamster balls.

Colin Hinchcliff longs for the touch of another human being. He can't handle the loneliness, the confinement, and he's horribly claustrophobic. The only thing keeping him going is his unrequited love for an exotic dancer named Siren, a woman who has never seen his face, doesn't even know his name. But when The Kill Ball, a serial slasher in a black leather sphere, begins targeting women at Siren's club, Colin decides he has to do whatever it takes in order to protect her... even if he has to break out of his bubble and risk everything to do it.

THE TICK PEOPLE

They call it Gloom Town, but that isn't its real name. It is a sad city, the saddest of cities, a place so utterly depressing that even their ales are brewed with the most sorrow-filled tears. They built it on the back of a colossal mountain-sized animal, where its woeful citizens live like human fleas within the hairy, pulsing landscape. And those tasked with keeping the city in a state of constant melancholy are the Stressmen—a team of professional sadness-makers who are perpetually striving to invent new ways of causing absolute misery.

But for the Stressman known as Fernando Mendez, creating grief hasn't been so easy as of late. His ideas aren't effective anymore. His treatments are more likely to induce happiness than sadness. And if he wants to get back in the game, he's going to have to relearn the true meaning of despair.

THE HAUNTED VAGINA

It's difficult to love a woman whose vagina is a gateway to the world of the dead...

Steve is madly in love with his eccentric girlfriend, Stacy. Unfortunately, their sex life has been suffering as of late, because Steve is worried about the odd noises that have been coming from Stacy's pubic region. She says that her vagina is haunted. She doesn't think it's that big of a deal. Steve, on the other hand, completely disagrees.

When a living corpse climbs out of her during an awkward night of sex, Stacy learns that her vagina is actually a doorway to another world. She persuades Steve to climb inside of her to explore this strange new place. But once inside, Steve finds it difficult to return... especially once he meets an oddly attractive woman named Fig, who lives within the lonely haunted world between Stacy's legs.

THE CANNIBALS OF CANDYLAND

There exists a race of cannibals who are made out of candy. They live in an underground world filled with lollipop forests and gumdrop goblins. During the day, while you are away at work, they come above ground and prowl our streets for food. Their prey: your children. They lure young boys and girls to them with their sweet scent and bright colorful candy coating, then rip them apart with razor sharp teeth and claws.

When he was a child, Franklin Pierce witnessed the death of his siblings at the hands of a candy woman with pink cotton candy hair. Since that day, the candy people have become his obsession. He has spent his entire life trying to prove that they exist. And after discovering the entrance to the underground world of the candy people, Franklin finds himself venturing into their sugary domain. His mission: capture one of them and bring it back, dead or alive.

THE EGG MAN

It is a survival of the fittest world where humans reproduce like insects, children are the property of corporations, and having a ten-foot tall brain is a grotesque sexual fetish.

Lincoln has just been released into the world by the Georges Organization, a corporation that raises creative types. A Smell, he has little prospect of succeeding as a visual artist. But after he moves into the Henry Building, he meets Luci, the weird and grimy girl who lives across the hall. She is a Sight. She is also the most disgusting woman Lincoln has ever met. Little does he know, she will soon become his muse.

Now Luci's boyfriend is threatening to kill Lincoln, two rival corporations are preparing for war, and Luci is dragging him along to discover the truth about the mysterious egg man who lives next door. Only the strongest will survive in this tale of individuality, love, and mutilation.

APESHIT

Apeshit is Mellick's love letter to the great and terrible B-horror movie genre. Six trendy teenagers (three cheerleaders and three football players) go to an isolated cabin in the mountains for a weekend of drinking, partying, and crazy sex, only to find themselves in the middle of a life and death struggle against a horribly mutated psychotic freak that just won't stay dead. Mellick parodies this horror cliché and twists it into something deeper and stranger. It is the literary equivalent of a grindhouse film. It is a splatter punk's wet dream. It is perhaps one of the most fucked up books ever written.

If you are a fan of Takashi Miike, Evil Dead, early Peter Jackson, or Eurotrash horror, then you must read this book.

CLUSTERFUCK

A bunch of douchebag frat boys get trapped in a cave with sub-terranean cannibal mutants and try to survive not by using their wits but by following the bro code...

From master of bizarro fiction Carlton Mellick III, author of the international cult hits Satan Burger and Adolf in Wonderland, comes a violent and hilarious B movie in book form. Set in the same woods as Mellick's splatterpunk satire Apeshit, Clusterfuck follows Trent Chesterton, alpha bro, who has come up with what he thinks is a flawless plan to get laid. He invites three hot chicks and his three best bros on a weekend of extreme cave diving in a remote area known as Turtle Mountain, hoping to impress the ladies with his expert caving skills.

But things don't quite go as Trent planned. For starters, only one of the three chicks turns out to be remotely hot and she has no interest in him for some inexplicable reason. Then he ends up looking like a total dumbass when everyone learns he's never actually gone caving in his entire life. And to top it all off, he's the one to get blamed once they find themselves lost and trapped deep underground with no way to turn back and no possible chance of rescue. What's a bro to do? Sure he could win some points if he actually tried to save the ladies from the family of unkillable subterranean cannibal mutants hunting them for their flesh, but fuck that. No slam piece is worth that amount of effort. He'd much rather just use them as bait so that he can save himself.

THE BABY JESUS BUTT PLUG

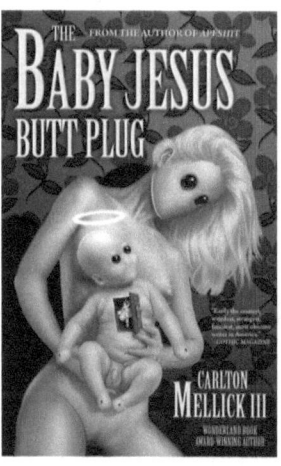

Step into a dark and absurd world where human beings are slaves to corporations, people are photocopied instead of born, and the baby jesus is a very popular anal probe.

SWEET STORY

Sally is an odd little girl. It's not because she dresses as if she's from the Edwardian era or spends most of her time playing with creepy talking dolls. It's because she chases rainbows as if they were butterflies. She believes that if she finds the end of the rainbow then magical things will happen to her--leprechauns will shower her with gold and fairies will grant her every wish. But when she actually does find the end of a rainbow one day, and is given the opportunity to wish for whatever she wants, Sally asks for something that she believes will bring joy to children all over the world. She wishes that it would rain candy forever. She had no idea that her innocent wish would lead to the extinction of all life on earth.

Sweet Story is a children's book gone horribly wrong. What starts as a cute, charming tale of rainbows and wishes soon becomes a vicious, unrelenting tale of survival in an inhospitable world full of cannibals and rapists. The result is one of the darkest comedies you'll read all year, told with the wit and style you've come to expect from a Mellick novel.

AS SHE STABBED ME GENTLY IN THE FACE

Oksana Maslovskiy is an award-winning artist, an internationally adored fashion model, and one of the most infamous serial killers this country has ever known. She enjoys murdering pretty young men with a nine-inch blade, cutting them open and admiring their delicate insides. It's the only way she knows how to be intimate with another human being. But one day she meets a victim who cannot be killed. His name is Gabriel—a mysterious immortal being with a deep desire to save Oksana's soul. He makes her a deal: if she promises to never kill another person again, he'll become her eternal murder victim.

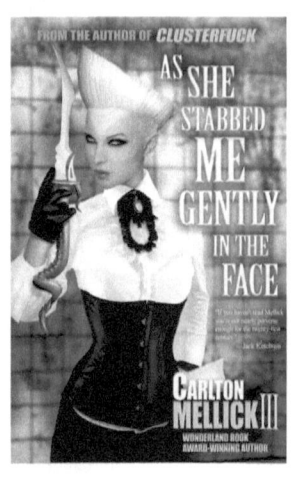

What at first seems like the perfect relationship for Oksana quickly devolves into a living nightmare when she discovers that Gabriel enjoys being killed by her just a little too much. He turns out to be obsessive, possessive, and paranoid that she might be murdering other men behind his back. And because he is unkillable, it's not going to be easy for Oksana to get rid of him.

TUMOR FRUIT

Eight desperate castaways find themselves stranded on a mysterious deserted island. They are surrounded by poisonous blue plants and an ocean made of acid. Ravenous creatures lurk in the toxic jungle. The ghostly sound of crying babies can be heard on the wind.

Once they realize the rescue ships aren't coming, the eight castaways must band together in order to survive in this inhospitable environment. But survival might not be possible. The air they breathe is lethal, there is no shelter from the elements, and the only food they have to consume is the colorful squid-shaped tumors that grow from a mentally disturbed woman's body.